"I've got a date tonight."

"You do?" Becca couldn't quite keep the excitement out of her voice, but Randi gave her full marks for effort. "Who with?"

"Zack Foster. He's the new partner at the veterinary clinic."

"Oh?"

Randi almost smiled at the eagerness her sister-in-law was trying so hard to conceal. Except that she felt so miserable, smiling wasn't currently an option. "I can't go," she muttered.

"Why not?" There was curiosity and concern in Becca's voice.

"I don't know," Randi admitted. "I've only met the man once, and he...he scares me."

"Zack? I've only seen him a couple of times and he's big, I'll grant you. But a teddy bear."

"It's not that Zack scares me, exactly," she said, staring down at the logo on her shoe. "When I was sitting in his office yesterday, it was almost like I'd been hypnotized. I was practically ready to agree to anything he said. It was the oddest sensation...."

Dear Reader,

I'm really glad you've decided to join me here in Shelter Valley. I've been visiting this town on and off for a while now, and I find it harder and harder to leave each time I have to return to my "other" world. There's so much going on here—so many great people, so many stories to tell....

Like the story of Randi Parsons and Zack Foster. Now, here are two interesting people. They're both attractive, successful, honest and hardworking—and they're both living at home at a time when they should be starting families. Because underneath all the smiles they have scars no one else can see. They touched me, I think, because they're like a lot of us who put on our smiles to face the world when deep inside there's pain most people never know about. Pain that sometimes attacks us in the middle of our busy days with no warning at all. Pain brought on by seemingly inconsequential things—a song on the radio, a phrase someone uses, a person who looks like someone we once knew.

I admire Randi in particular because she won't compromise who she is, even when that person won't fit the stereotypes people expect her to fit. She'd rather be alone—forcing herself to be happy—than lose the person who lives inside her. She makes no apologies for her differences, while accepting extreme differences in those around her. She's a fighter. And a dreamer. A difficult combination. But a great one, too.

And Zack...well, I'm pretty certain he'll make your heart beat faster if nothing else. He's my idea of a hero. He's sexy, athletic, logical, capable and he has a huge heart. Many parts of my own true-life hero slipped in here when I wasn't looking.

So...enjoy. And don't worry. I've so enjoyed my time in Shelter Valley that I'm coming back soon! I hope you will, too.

Tara Taylor Quinn

I love to hear from readers. You can reach me at: P.O. Box 15065, Scottsdale, Arizona 85267-5065 or online at http://www.inficad.com/~ttquinn

White Picket Fences
Tara Taylor Quinn

HARLEQUIN®

TORONTO • NEW YORK • LONDON
AMSTERDAM • PARIS • SYDNEY • HAMBURG
STOCKHOLM • ATHENS • TOKYO • MILAN • MADRID
PRAGUE • WARSAW • BUDAPEST • AUCKLAND

ISBN 0-373-70954-4

WHITE PICKET FENCES

Thanks to the faculty and staff in the men's and women's athletic departments at Scottsdale Community College, Scottsdale, Arizona. Any accurate portrayals of life in the academic sports world must be attributed to them. Any mistakes are my own.

Dedication:

For my mother, Penny Gumser,
who gave me life.
And for my editor, Paula Eykelhof,
who brings my dreams to life.
I couldn't have done this without either one of you.

CHAPTER ONE

SOMETHING WAS MISSING.

Trailing through her house, leaving lights on in her wake, Miranda Parsons frowned. Why did she have this odd empty feeling?

She'd painted her living room last summer; she'd bought a luscious daybed ensemble with matching everything for her spare bedroom over Thanksgiving. And now, during Christmas break, she'd given the kitchen a coat of yellow paint, papered the wall in the breakfast alcove with wildflowers and hung curtains.

Her little house was finally done as she'd envisioned when she'd bought it eighteen months before. She should be feeling satisfied. Complete.

Making her way down the hall, she scrutinized the master bedroom and en suite bathroom carefully for anything amiss. The maroon comforter and pillow shams, the plush towels in the bathroom, the hand-woven tapestry rug on the bedroom floor were all as they should be. As she wanted them.

She loved this house.

So what was missing?

It was Tuesday morning, the second of January.

She had another week off before she had to report back to school, once again taking up her position as women's athletic director at the university. Though she'd been hoping to get to Phoenix for several rounds of golf with some friends, it was equally important to make sure her living space was just right. She could do more here if she needed to.

If only the place would speak up, tell her what to do. There certainly wasn't anyone else here to give her any suggestions.

Randi wandered outside. Shelter Valley's blue skies and sunshine she took for granted, though she loved them, too. Even a temperature of 65 degrees in January was a given. The tiny patch of grass in her front yard was as green and verdant as it should be. The stucco finish on the house looked great.

Sitting on the boulder in her front yard—a costly bit of landscaping she was very happy with—Randi folded her arms and surveyed her property. Yep. She was still certain the place suited her.

So why in hell didn't she feel *complete?*

She could get a pet. Except that she thought they were mostly nuisances.

Or a roommate. Yuck.

Maybe she needed Surround Sound. She was no electrician, but surely one of her brothers could be prevailed upon for his expertise. There had to be some benefit in putting up with the four of them.

Will was out—he was too busy being important at

the university. And spending every spare minute of his life with his adorable baby girl.

Randi was spending a lot of spare minutes with the little miracle herself.

So maybe Paul could help her. He'd rewired his attic a few years ago. Surround Sound might be just the ticket.

Except she didn't *really* want it. She was perfectly happy with her stereo system. She had digital cable television, too.

Her neighbor passed by, walking her dog. The little thing peed on the edge of Randi's fertilized grass.

Maybe she needed a fence.

Yeah.

Looking around the perimeter of her front yard, noticing how it ran right off to the sidewalk without so much as a by-your-leave, she nodded. That was it. When she was growing up, she'd always had this image of a home with a picket fence. Probably got it from watching too many reruns of *The Donna Reed Show* or *Leave It to Beaver.*

Heaving a sigh of relief, Randi slid off her boulder and went back inside. Thank goodness that was settled. She probably didn't have time this break to install a fence, which was fine with her; she could go to Phoenix and play as good a round of golf as she was still capable of playing.

But come spring break, she'd get this done.

All her life needed was a white picket fence.

HE'D MADE IT through New Year's. Zack Foster heated up a frozen dinner Tuesday night, feeling rather proud of himself. He'd taken a dose of his own medicine—let the animals he cared for ease him into the barren new year. Pet therapy.

He'd spent New Year's Eve with the boarders at the veterinary clinic, giving his employees the night off to be with family and friends. He'd walked the dogs, scratched the cats' ears, thrown balls and given treats, filled bowls and water bottles, and graciously accepted his due of kisses and purrs.

Whistling as he pulled the foil off his steaming lasagna, he reflected on the previous day, pleased to know, firsthand, that the program he'd dedicated a good portion of his career to really worked. Animals, simply through their unconditional—and sometimes unsolicited—affection, could ease the burdens of human beings.

New Year's Day, he'd been on duty, taking the emergency cases at the clinic—a dog hit by a car, a bird with a broken wing, a cat with a bleeding paw— so that his partner, Cassie Tate, could go to Phoenix with her parents and two youngest sisters to spend the day with her uncle and his family.

Yes, he'd done well. Was damn proud of himself. As a matter of fact, now that he'd made it through the last of the holidays, he deserved a beer.

A bit of tomato sauce dripped from the foil he'd removed from his dinner and plopped on the ceramic tile of his kitchen floor. Ignoring it, Zack deposited the foil in the trash and grabbed a beer from the refrigerator.

By the time he'd opened the bottle, the floor was clean. Thanks to Sammie, his canine garbage disposal.

"Good girl, Sam," Zack praised the Sheltie. Sam wagged her tail, turned a circle and barked. Hearing her, Bear, his fifteen-year-old poodle-Pomeranian mix, trudged out to the kitchen to see what he'd missed. His chocolate-colored body seemed to move more slowly every day.

"Here you go, boy," he said, dropping a bite of lasagna on the floor beneath Bear's nose. And then, while the dog lapped heartily, he asked, "How's that new arthritis medicine working?"

Bear licked his chops and, staring up at Zack, lay down right where he was.

"You're all right, Bear, my man," Zack said, testing the lasagna himself. "You've got a healthy heart, and we'll find something that makes those bones of yours more willing to serve you."

He took a swig of beer. And another. He'd had Bear since he was in high school. Didn't look forward to the day when his pal would no longer be lying at his feet, silent but loyal company.

Lasagna long gone, kitchen cleaned and three beer bottles emptied, Zack took his fourth bottle out back to his patio and the seven-foot deep pool in his backyard. Sammie trotted at his heels, her mouth open in the smile she wore much of the time. Bear followed more slowly.

Flipping the switch beside the pump, Zack turned on the lights by the pool. The pool was heated; he could get in if he wanted to. But he didn't feel much like swimming. After a long couple of weeks at the clinic, he really just wanted to sit.

Zack lounged in one of the two chaise longues that had been just about his only furniture for the first six months he'd owned this house. He didn't move, except to retrieve another beer—and then the entire twelve-pack to save himself another trip in. Stars were out; he could look for the big dipper.

"It's not you, Zack, it's me...."

Dawn's pretty face swam before his eyes, her intelligent compassionate voice ringing in his ears.

Zack shook his head, blinked until the lighted water in front of him came back into focus.

He didn't need to relive it all again. He'd been over everything so many times it was mush. There was no point in revisiting any of this—ever. He'd looked at the breakup of his marriage from angles that mathematicians didn't even know existed.

And the facts never changed.

It was why he'd come to Shelter Valley. To forget Dawn. To get away from the constant memories.

And because he'd been intrigued by Cassie's offer of a partnership. Her timing had been impeccable.

He took another swig of beer. All he wanted was to relax. Maybe fall asleep out here, where the night air would keep him cool, where there were no walls to close him in.

The house he and Dawn had owned in Phoenix was spacious, full of windows. Sammie and Bear had had a huge backyard filled with luscious grass and their own doggie door to let themselves in and out. Dawn had insisted on that for the summer months, when it was too hot to leave them outside all day while they were both at work. She'd sure loved the dogs.

Maybe they should've had children. She'd said she wasn't ready. And Lord knew Zack had his plate full, as well, working in one of the largest veterinary clinics in the city. But maybe if she'd had children at home...

Zack shook his head again, then took another swig of beer.

And he remembered...

"ZACK, WE NEED TO TALK."

He came more fully into the bedroom, watching as Dawn zipped up the back of her chic navy-blue dress. He thought of offering to help, but knew that if he did, neither one of them would get to work on time.

"What's up?" he asked her. She'd been out late the night before, another dinner meeting. Dawn was an advertising executive and often worked late in the evenings.

"I just need to talk to you about something."

"Can it wait until tonight?" he asked, leaning against the doorjamb even though he really needed to leave if he was going to make his eight-o'clock appointment to spay Mrs. Andrews's new beagle. But he was enjoying the view, watching as Dawn put on her earrings, clasped her watch around her wrist. Applied lip liner and then lipstick. She was one of the most feminine women he'd ever met, and after living almost thirty years with his own large athletic body, he was fascinated by the contrast between the two of them.

He'd had lovers before Dawn, feminine women who complemented his masculinity, but none of them had captivated him as much as she had.

He tried to meet her eyes in the mirror over her dresser, but she was obviously preoccupied.

She turned to face him and Zack straightened as she finally met his eyes. "No, it can't wait," she said. Her tone was serious. "I promised myself I'd do this now, and if I don't, I'm not sure when I will."

This didn't sound like a dinner engagement she'd forgotten to mention. Something was wrong. His muscles tensed as he waited.

He'd never known Dawn to have problems talking to him before.

"I want a divorce."

He fell back a step as the words hit him, but they didn't really register.

"What?"

"I want a divorce. I'm going to file today."

"What?" Same word, a little louder. Still no comprehension.

"I know this is hard, coming out of the blue, but you have no idea how long I've been thinking about it, and now that I know for sure, I just have to do it and get it done." She was talking so fast he could hardly keep up with her.

Mrs. Andrews's beagle was going to have another day, another chance.

Zack took a deep breath. "What's wrong?" he asked. If only he could get to the root of this problem he hadn't even known he had. He was sure they could fix it, whatever it was. He and Dawn were great together. Their relationship worked smoothly, and they solved problems by consensus. They compromised easily, hardly ever disagreeing.

They were a good pair. A team.

Just look at the beautiful house they owned and ran together. Their well-organized lives. The dogs they both adored.

Her eyes lifted, met his again. He glimpsed the pain in them, the regret, and started to feel sick.

"I can change." He said the first thing that came to mind, idiotic though it was. Not that he wasn't willing to do whatever he could to save his marriage, but he had no idea what was even bothering her.

Maybe she hated Phoenix, wanted to move. Maybe she'd had a job offer somewhere far away—like Massachusetts. He'd hate to give up his practice, his patients, but he would. He'd hate the cold weather, too. The snow. But he'd adjust.

She'd do the same for him if the situation were reversed.

They were a team. Comfortable. Part of the same whole.

"It's not you, Zack," she said, her voice breaking as she turned away, fumbled with the diamond tennis bracelet he'd bought her for their fifth anniversary.

"What is it?" he asked again, standing upright, his muscular frame leaving barely any space in the doorway. He had some crazy notion of blocking her escape should she try to leave before she came to her senses, before he helped her work this out. But he knew that if she pushed past him, he'd let her go.

He had to. They were equals. A team.

His pager went off. Zack ignored it. His staff would be worried; he never missed an appointment. But for once, they'd have to wait. They'd understand.

Dawn stopped fiddling with her jewelry and Zack approached her slowly, taking her slim shoulders in his hands. "Talk to me, honey," he said. "I know we haven't spent much time together in the past year or two…" Make that five or six. "We've both been so busy getting established, but we're there now. We can finally afford to slow down a little bit, take those trips we always talked about."

She shook her head, cutting him off. When Zack looked up, he saw tears in her eyes.

"There's someone else," she whispered.

Jerking his hands away from her, he backed up a step. "You've slept with another man?"

The thought had never even occurred to him. She was his wife.

"No." She shook her head.

Thank God.

"Where would I ever find a man better-looking than you?" she asked, giving him an intimate little smile through her tears.

"Indeed," he agreed, because she seemed to expect it. He'd certainly never had troubles attracting women—the best-looking women. But he wasn't foolish enough to think that looks were all that mattered in a relationship. Far from it.

"I knew this was going to be hard," she whispered, still standing there by her dresser, watching him. "But I had no idea it was going to be this hard."

"Dawn, for God's sake, tell me what's wrong." He couldn't ever remember being so tense. Wasn't sure how much longer he could stand there calmly discussing things that made no sense.

"I'm in love with someone else."

But she'd just told him there *was* no one else. He was the best-looking man she'd ever seen.

"Who?"

She turned away, and something inside Zack cracked wide open.

"Barbara Sharp."

He frowned, his head spinning. He had to be missing large parts of this conversation.

"The golfer?" he asked. Zack didn't follow the game, but the Sharp woman was a local and had been in the news a lot lately.

Dawn nodded.

"But..."

Zack swallowed. Suddenly wanted to be anywhere but here. Anywhere but in this house—their house.

As the air grew almost too thick to breathe, Zack refused to utter the words screaming inside him. They were so incomprehensible he couldn't even say them.

Dawn finally turned toward him.

"But she's a woman." The words came, anyway. Zack wanted to snatch them back.

More so when he saw the pathetic glow in his wife's eyes as she nodded again.

CHAPTER TWO

ZACK TOOK ANOTHER SIP of beer, tried to clear his head, to send himself on another path. But the words and pictures just kept coming.

"But she's a woman." He'd said the words so innocently, as though his wife didn't know damn well what she was asking him to accept. Even now, after almost a year, he still couldn't believe that his wife had left him for a woman. That the woman he'd slept with for six years was more attracted to her own sex than she was to him.

He finished his beer in one long gulp and opened another.

In spite of making every effort not to fall in to the trap, he was back there again, seeing that glow in her eyes...

HE REELED BACK, feeling as though he'd been sucker punched. He *had* been sucker punched.

"I'm so sorry," Dawn said, her voice barely audible as her tears started to fall in earnest. "You don't know how hard I've fought this, but I just can't fight anymore."

There were a million things he didn't say. Accusations. Questions. Zack couldn't speak. Couldn't even think clearly enough to string coherent thoughts together. He could only stand there and stare at his sweet feminine wife. And wait.

Wait for her to do something. To take back the things she'd just said. Things that were too terrible to bear.

"Last night Barbara asked me to move in with her, and I can't tell her no, Zack. I want to be with her, to share her life more than anything I've ever wanted before. Suddenly things feel right—peaceful. When I'm with her, I feel…complete."

It just kept getting worse. "How long have you been seeing her?"

"A while."

"How long?" He was sure it didn't matter, but he had to focus on something before he crawled right out of his skin.

"I met her last year at the Phoenix Open."

She'd been there as a company sponsor, schmoozing in a VIP booth.

"You've been seeing her for more than a year?" He thought of all the nights he'd made love to her in the past fourteen months.

"For a long time we were just friends."

"Define 'long time.'"

"I don't know. Six months, maybe."

Which left eight unaccounted for. He nodded, clenching his jaw so hard it ached.

"Then, one night after we'd gone to a movie, she

asked me if I wanted to stop by her place for a drink...."

"I don't want to hear this." He ordered himself to vacate the premises, but his damn feet wouldn't move. There was going to be a punch line here somewhere. He just had to wait for it.

"She came out to me that night..."

"What does that mean?" The words were clipped, but they were the best he could do.

"She told me she was interested in having a relationship with me and asked me if that was something I would consider."

"Friendship wasn't relationship enough?" he muttered sarcastically. His world was out of control and he couldn't seem to stop it from spinning faster and faster.

"I know this is hard for you to understand—"

"Damn straight it's hard," he interrupted. "Try impossible."

Dawn sank down onto their bed, and as much as he wanted to hate her, Zack had to admire the way she was sticking this out. Trying to do the decent thing by him. Some distant part of Zack even appreciated the attention she was giving him.

"I'm in love with her," she said, shaking her head helplessly.

"We're talking about a *woman* here!"

"I know." Her face lined with confusion, she sounded as though she was finding it as difficult to make sense of all this as he was. Except that she'd apparently had a lot longer to get used to the idea. Eight months, to be exact.

Zack turned away. He couldn't even look at the bed he'd shared with her during the past eight months. Couldn't think of all the times he'd made love to her.

Oh, God. He felt sicker than ever. Had she been thinking of another woman whenever he'd...

"How does a woman suddenly decide she wants another woman?" he demanded, feeling frustrated. Hurt.

"I suspected I might be a lesbian even before we got married."

"You had relationships with other women way back then?" He swung around to pin her with an accusing glare. How in hell could he not have known?

"No." She shook her head, withstood his look. "I could never quite acknowledge that there were just times when I'd feel something—or more importantly, *wouldn't* feel something."

That punched him in the gut. "You were faking the whole time you were with me?"

"No!" She stood, approached him, stopping only when he started to back away from her. "That's just it. When I met you, when you touched me, I felt real desire for a man for the first time in my life. I can't tell you how relieved I was."

Zack held out a hand to her. "Then..."

She shook her head, forestalling his words. "It

didn't last,'' she said. ''Or at least, not strongly enough. I feel things when I'm with Barbara that I've never felt before. This is right for me, Zack. I'm one hundred percent sure of it.''

There appeared to be nothing left to say. Hands in his slacks pockets, Zack wondered how best to extricate himself, pride intact.

''I care very much for you, Zack,'' she said beseechingly. He couldn't figure out why she'd bothered to say that.

''Not enough, apparently.''

''Plenty,'' she countered. ''More than you'll ever know. It's killing me to do this.''

''Then don't do it.'' So much for pride. ''Let's just forget this whole conversation ever took place.''

But could he really? Every time he looked at her he'd have to picture her with—

''I just don't feel anything...sexually when I'm with you.''

He felt the blood drain from his face.

''I want more than anything to be your friend.''

''I don't think that'll be possible.'' The cold voice that said those words wasn't one he even recognized.

Dawn bowed her head. ''I understand.''

''Do you?'' the stranger's voice continued.

''Yes,'' she whispered, fresh tears pooling in her soft blue eyes as she looked up at him. ''Please, please don't blame yourself for this,'' she begged him, touching his arm.

Zack jerked away. ''Who else am I to blame when

my wife tells me that I'm not only unable to keep her happy in our bed, I can't manage to keep her at all? That she doesn't want to be married to me because...because I'm the wrong sex. If that makes any sense.''

"I had the...tendencies before I ever met you, Zack.''

"But I was able to change that. To turn you on.''

"For a brief time, yes.'' She nodded.

"Maybe if I'd been man enough, the time wouldn't have been so brief.'' His own voice was back—sort of. It was thick with emotion. Saying things he couldn't stomach.

"If you hadn't been such an incredible man, I would never have felt anything to begin with.''

"Perhaps that would have been better.''

"Perhaps. For you, at least.''

He glanced over at her, wondering what she meant by that.

"I'll never be sorry that I knew you Zack. You've added dimensions to my life that I'll cherish forever.''

He didn't need any of her sap for his battered pride. He didn't need anything from her.

He knew what she was saying. Understood that he wasn't to blame for Dawn's choices. But deep down in his gut, he still *felt* responsible. Somehow.

"I'll be gone tonight,'' he told her, striding for the door.

"You'll need time to arrange for movers and—''

"I don't want a damn thing from this house," he said, "except Sammie and Bear. They're mine." That was the only thing he was sure of. "You can have it all—sell it all—I don't give a damn what you do with it...."

A wet nose nudged Zack's palm, brought him back to the present. He ignored it. He still didn't give a damn. It was the only way to get from one day to the next. Because you couldn't take anything for granted. Not even something as basic as love and marriage. One minute it was there, and the very next minute, reality could completely change.

The only given was himself.

The nose nudged him again. Harder.

Looking into Sammie's big dark eyes, Zack sighed, setting down the bottle he still clutched in one hand. Hell.

He'd gone and done it, anyway—he'd thought of Dawn. Relived that whole last horrible scene—for the first time in weeks.

He'd wallowed.

And he hated that.

"Okay, Sammie, my girl, from now on, we play catch in the evenings, got it?" he asked.

She wagged her tail, turned in a circle and barked.

Now *there* was one female he could count on.

IN DEFERENCE TO the cooler sixty-degree temperature, Randi pulled a sweatshirt over the usual bike shorts and cropped T-shirt she wore to work. And added the finishing touch, the sports socks and tennis shoes that were also standard attire for the youngest women's athletic director Montford University had ever had. Classes didn't start for another week—the fifteenth of January—but Randi, along with the rest of the Montford faculty, was due back the Monday before.

Not a minute too soon, as far as she was concerned.

Running her fingers through her short blond hair, she dashed for her Jeep. She had a meeting later that morning with her head basketball coach—recruitment possibilities to discuss—but Randi had something else to accomplish first. Something to knock off her list—she hoped.

The Shelter Valley Veterinary Clinic was just around the corner from downtown, not even a block from Main Street. The newish-looking structure was familiar to Randi, but only from a drive-by position. She'd never had reason to visit it before.

And hoped never to have reason to visit it again.

What could Will have been thinking, giving her this assignment? He had to know she'd try to unload it.

Which might very well have been his plan. Cancel the whole thing. Who ever heard of a university having a pet-therapy club, anyway?

Parking the Jeep, Randi hopped out and latched the door behind her. She could just picture it, a bunch of dogs in private offices, sitting in armchairs in front of couches, administering therapy to emotionally disturbed people.

Shaking her head, she entered the building. Cassie Tate had opened the clinic almost three years before, but from what Randi had heard, she wasn't in town all that much now that she was teaching the rest of the country about pet therapy. Randi had gone to school with Cassie, and while they hadn't been particularly close—Cassie had only had eyes, and time, for Sam Montford, and Randi had already been in training for her stint with the Ladies Professional Golf Association—Randi had always respected Cassie.

"Can I help you?" a young college student asked from her position behind the reception counter.

"Sure," Randi said, glancing around the waiting room as she approached. One woman with a cat. In a carrier. "Is Dr. Foster around?"

"Zack?"

"Yeah."

"Do you have an appointment?" The girl looked down at the book in front of her and then over the counter to notice Randi's lack of a pet.

"No," she said. She'd been hoping to just pop in and make this short and sweet. Emphasis on short.

"Can I tell him who's here?"

"Randi Parsons. I'm from the university, and I need to speak with him about the pet-therapy club."

The girl nodded and pushed through a swinging door behind her.

Okay, Randi understood the part about extracurricular activities on campus and even the fact that she had to be an adviser. She'd managed to avoid it so far, although most of the Montford faculty served eventually. It kept the teachers and students unified, working toward common goals. Many of the activities were community-oriented, which helped solidify the values of which Montford was so proud. She was for all of that. Would lobby for it, if necessary.

But *pet* therapy?

"You can go on back." The receptionist had returned. "He's in his office, third door on the right."

"Thanks," Randi said, rounding the counter with her fingers crossed. Five minutes should make all the difference.

She'd seen Dr. Zack Foster from a distance. In a town the size of Shelter Valley, it was pretty much impossible not to at least catch a glimpse of each of the two thousand or so permanent residents at some time or other. Even if said resident had been in town for less than a year. There was only one major grocery store, two gas stations, one real restaurant. Everyone was seen eventually.

Besides, Zack Foster was a basketball fan. She'd noticed him at one of the final women's games when Montford had been on its way to the championship.

Which they'd won. Randi still felt a little glow of pride when she thought about it.

Seeing him from a distance was nothing like being

in the same room with him. Up close he was huge. Not an ounce overweight, just muscular. Solid.

"Dr. Foster?"

"Please, call me Zack." He rose and offered her his hand.

Randi swallowed. "I'm Randi Parsons." Her voice almost cracked.

What the hell was the matter with her?

"Good to meet you," he said, looking at her oddly. "I followed Montford's women's basketball last season. Very impressive."

"Thanks."

She'd been around big men all her life. Had four of them for older brothers, and ever since she'd been able to walk she'd been able to take on all four of them with one hand tied behind her back. Both hands, if it came to that.

He didn't sit back down. Didn't offer her a seat, either, not that she planned to stay long. At least she didn't *think* she planned to. He had the bluest eyes she'd ever seen. And they were boring holes in her.

"Uh, do I, uh, have jelly smeared on my mouth?" she asked, wiping her lips even though she hadn't had jelly in years. Or breakfast that morning, for that matter.

"No, of course not." His gaze dropped. "Sorry about that. Please, have a seat."

Randi sat. She had the strangest feeling that she'd do just about anything the man asked of her right then. A feeling she'd never had before in her life. One she hoped never to have again.

"I, uh, just wanted to speak with you a moment about Montford's pet-therapy club. I was told you're administering it from the professional side."

"I am." He nodded, one thumb busy thumping a folder on top of his desk.

The man was having the most discomforting effect on Randi. She had no idea what to do with it. Her only consolation was that he seemed to be just as uncomfortable as she was.

Good. That should make it even easier to accomplish her task.

"I've been assigned to be the club's faculty adviser."

"What happened to Dr. Randolph?"

"He retired."

"Oh."

The vet's blue eyes were studying her again, as though he saw something he didn't know what to do with, either.

She'd help him out. Help them both out.

"The thing is, I know Cassie's made quite a name for herself with her pet therapy, helping emotionally disturbed people and all, but this club, it can't have any real impact. The kids running it aren't trained like Cassie is. Nor am I. We don't have the psychology background."

"There are many kinds of pet therapy—"

"I'm just thinking that, with Cassie being out of

town so much and you having to carry an extra load, we'd be remiss not to understand your commitments and cancel the club, at least for this semester. Let you off the hook, so to speak.''

''I don't want to be let off the hook, but thank you for your consideration.'' If she wasn't mistaken, his words held just a bit of mockery. As though he knew she hadn't really been thinking of him at all.

Or, at least, only as an afterthought.

Randi wanted out of this assignment. More than ever, now that she was actually sitting here with Zack Foster. His glance was so powerful, something about him so compelling, her stomach was almost quivering.

Her stomach never quivered.

''What good are a bunch of untutored college kids going to be?'' she asked, determined to do what she'd come here to do and get the hell out of there. ''I don't imagine they can learn enough about therapy in the five short meetings allotted to us.''

''They don't need any training at all,'' Zack said with great confidence. ''And the meetings aren't all that short. We take four or five trips a semester into Phoenix to nursing homes there. I provide the dogs, you provide the dogs' partners, whose only job it is to take the dogs into different rooms and let them do their stuff.''

He lost Randi with the remark about meetings that weren't short. She had a very full schedule this semester. She had a new cross-country coach to stay on top of and a budget that wasn't going to stretch all the way. Plus, the athletic conference of which Montford was a part was completely reworking its policies this spring. And in her spare time, her focus had to be on recruiting for the basketball team so they weren't a one-season wonder. She needed the gate money or she'd have to consider cutting the women's gymnastics program.

Men's gymnastics had already been cut to give women's athletics a more equitable financial share.

"This is all very altruistic," she said, knowing she should be stating her case more strongly—even while her tongue failed to do so. "But do you really think it's worth the effort to take a bunch of kids into Phoenix when your time—and mine—is at such a premium?" She didn't want to waste four or five afternoons on something as frivolous as pet therapy, but neither did she want to bring a frown to that face. She didn't want to earn Zack Foster's disregard.

Which made no sense at all. She hadn't cowered before a man's displeasure her entire life. A woman in athletics couldn't afford to let men intimidate her. She'd never get anywhere. Randi lived in a man's world and could hold her own with the best of them.

"I take it you aren't thrilled with this appointment," Zack drawled, a half smile on his face.

"Let's just say I don't have time to waste," she answered curtly. It was the best comeback she could manage.

And it wasn't all that good.

CHAPTER THREE

"WHAT MAKES YOU so sure the pet-therapy club would be a waste of time?"

She threw up a hand. "What's an animal going to do for some frail old person that modern science and medication isn't already doing? Except bring germs into an already fragile environment? Or scare them half to death."

He sat back, hands steepled under his chin. "Germs?"

She was not going to be intimidated. His opinion of her mattered not at all. Her *time* did.

"Everyone knows that dogs, you know, lick themselves."

"Yeah."

"In, uh, inappropriate places."

"They also have the cleanest mouths of just about any creature, including human beings. They excrete a natural antiseptic which is why, when they lick a wound, it heals faster."

She hadn't known that—exactly—but it still didn't change her mind. "So how many old people need wounds licked?"

"It might also interest you to know," he continued

as though she hadn't even spoken, "that it's been scientifically proved that petting an animal—a dog—reduces blood pressure in people."

He was a veterinarian. He'd dedicated his life to caring for beasts. He was supposed to say stuff like that. "So does medi—"

"Pets also provide relief from depression—a disease that abounds in nursing homes."

Nothing a good psychiatrist couldn't do.

"Listen, I'll be honest with you," she said. "I just don't have the time this semester to chase off to Phoenix on the off chance that we'll find some depressed old person with high blood pressure. An old person, moreover, who *wants* his privacy invaded by a college kid and a dog." Put that way, the project sounded as invalid as she believed it to be.

He shrugged. "So get someone else to take your place."

Didn't he think she'd already tried that? "I can't." Having your brother as president of the university for which you worked definitely had its drawbacks.

"You've never had a pet, have you?" His smile slid all the way through her. Her legs were a little shaky now, too. Must be hunger. She had an energy bar out in her glove compartment that was calling to her.

"No." And she didn't want a pet. All that hair and slobber. Ugh. It gave her the willies just thinking about it.

Besides, dogs bit. Randi shuddered.

"This is probably a little forward, but I'd like a chance to convince you how worthwhile this program is. Will you have dinner with me tomorrow night?"

"Yes."

No. I meant no.

"It's a date, then." He stood up before Randi could tell him she'd said the wrong word. She didn't date. Before she could tell him she'd changed her mind, he said, "I'll pick you up at six, if that's okay with you. We can drive into Phoenix."

A date. She didn't remember how to go on a date. It'd been years since she'd even tried.

She had to tell him she'd said yes but meant no.

Somehow, Randi found herself back in her Jeep with absolutely nothing accomplished. The man had the strangest effect on her. She was still stuck with pet therapy. And there was another pressing problem on her horizon, as well.

She had twenty-four hours to find something to wear.

IT TOOK ABOUT ten minutes to wipe the smile off Zack's face. What the hell was he doing?

So Randi Parsons was an attractive package. Her sexy long legs in those tight black shorts had been enough to wind him. And she was smart and sassy, too. But he'd been with several attractive intelligent women in the ten months since Dawn had filed for divorce. Had enjoyed them very much. He wasn't in any way desperate for an attractive woman.

And he could sure as hell find one who offered a lot more promise—a lot less aggravation—than Randi Parsons. The woman hated animals.

And she was an athlete. Just like Barbara Sharp.

What did that make him? A masochist?

BECAUSE HE'D PLAYED CATCH with Sammie every night for the past five nights and the poor girl deserved a rest, Zack stopped by Ben and Tory Sanders's apartment, instead. He had a sample bag of dog food for Buddy—the dog he'd talked Ben into adopting when the young man had first come to Shelter Valley the previous fall—and a free pass for Ben's seven-year-old daughter, Alex, to take horseback riding lessons. The owner of the stable was a client of Zack's.

"You two are looking good," he said to his friends, married almost a month now, as he sat across from them in the living room. They were sitting about as close as they could sit without actually touching. Alex was in their bedroom, playing a video game that Tory had hooked up to their television for her.

Tory looked at Ben, smiled and then looked down.

"We're doing great," Ben said. "Thanks for the riding lessons," he said, his eyes forthright as they met Zack's. "You didn't have to do that."

"It was nothing." The stable owner had been

more than happy to pay part of his monthly bill with the lessons.

"Consider it rental payments for your truck all those times last fall when you drove me into Phoenix to pick up my furniture," Zack told his friend.

"You got the whole place furnished yet?" Ben asked with a grin.

"Just about." Zack took a sip of the lemonade Tory had served him. "The spare bedroom is still empty, and the office needs more than a desk, but otherwise, I'm done."

Buddy came in from the bedroom, sniffed Zack's shoes and then hopped into his lap.

"Buddy, down," Ben ordered.

Buddy lay in Ben's lap.

"Buddy, get down," Tory said softly.

Buddy dropped to the floor and ambled over to lie down at Tory's feet.

"It's clear who's the boss around here," Zack teased his friend.

Ben leaned over, scratching the dog's ears. "It's about time to try those obedience classes again."

"Not if you're taking him," Tory said with a grin. "Leave him to Alex and me."

Zack didn't know Tory all that well, not only because she was relatively new to town, but because she was one of the most private people he'd ever met. Yet he couldn't help liking her. She'd sure made Ben a happy man.

And she'd taken on Ben's seven-year-old daughter, as well. That said a lot.

"So what's going on with Tory and Montford U?" Zack asked a few minutes later when they'd all three grown quiet.

Tory had spent the previous semester posing as her sister, teaching classes at the university when she didn't even have a college degree herself. She'd been driven to this desperate act by her abusive ex-husband, who'd murdered her sister, thinking he'd killed Tory. She was safe only as long as he believed her dead. He couldn't tolerate the thought of her having a life without him. Eventually he'd committed suicide, and all the deception had come to an end.

"They aren't pressing charges," Tory said, no trace of a smile left on her face.

"Thank God." Zack had been keeping his fingers crossed for his friends since he'd first heard the tragic story.

"That's not all," Ben added, with a glance at his wife. "They've given Tory a full scholarship to get her degree."

"Congratulations!"

"Thanks." Tory looked up at Ben, smiling, though her eyes were shadowed. "It's still kind of hard to take in."

"Won't some of the students who sat in your class last semester wonder why you're sitting in class with them now?"

Ben nodded. "The university is going to come out

with the whole story—or an abridged version of it—
the first week of class. Tory and I have already
proofed the copy. They did a really nice job. It'll be
published in the university newspaper, so everyone'll
have a chance to read the story. That way they won't
ask too many questions—we hope."

Zack nodded, fully aware that there was much of
Tory's background he didn't know, might never
know, but certain that she deserved these breaks, and
more.

He glanced down the hall toward the master bedroom, making sure that Ben's daughter wasn't on her
way in.

"Any word on Alex?" he asked. Ben was in the
process of trying to adopt Alex. Though he'd raised
her from the day she was born, believed her to be
his, had his name on her birth certificate, he'd found
out the previous year that he wasn't Alex's father at
all.

He'd lost her for a time to her real father, an ex-
con who'd taken his belt to the little girl. Ben had
gotten her back right before Christmas.

Ben shook his head.

"These things take time," Tory said, her hand
reaching for her husband. "We've been in almost
constant contact with the social worker and a nurse
from Alex's old school. Everything looks really
promising."

"She's a very lucky—"

Zack's words were interrupted by a knock on the door.

"Who could that be?" Tory asked, frowning up at Ben.

Zack turned to see as his younger friend opened the door. He didn't recognize the older, well-dressed couple standing there.

"Yes?" Ben asked politely.

"Are you Ben Sanders?" the man asked. His face was lined but looked friendly. The woman's lips seemed to be trembling.

"Yes," Ben answered immediately. "What can I do for you?"

Zack wondered if these people had something to do with Alex, maybe grandparents from her mother's side. They'd better not be there to take the child away from Ben and Tory.

"We're James and Carol Montford," the older gentleman said, his voice hoarse. The aunt and uncle Ben had never met.

"He looks so much like the pictures of Grace," Carol said to her husband, her eyes tearing up as she stared at Ben. "And like our Sam."

That would be Samuel Montford IV, Cassie's bastard of an ex-husband and the town founder's namesake. Zack could only imagine what Ben must be feeling, finally meeting these people who were his only living family. Family meant everything to Ben, and until a few months before, he'd thought himself alone in the world.

Zack stood up.

"Won't you come in?" Tory asked graciously, standing up, too.

On hearing her voice, Ben turned, glanced back at Tory. His eyes were blazing with emotion.

"Yes, please come in," he finally said, pulling the door wider as he stepped aside. "It's...I—"

"We won't stay long," Carol said gently. "We just couldn't wait any longer to meet you."

"We've been away," Ben explained, showing them to the couch he and Tory had been sharing a short time before. "After the holidays Tory, Alex and I went back to California to get the rest of Alex's belongings."

The Montfords glanced curiously at Tory. "This is our new niece we've heard so much about?" Carol asked.

"Yes." Ben drew Tory forward, though he released her almost immediately. "This is my wife, Tory."

"It's so nice to meet you," Tory said, her tone reflecting the manners she'd learned as the wife of one of the richest men on the East Coast. Zack half expected to see her curtsy.

"It's nice to meet you, too, dear. Better than nice. The Parsons have told me about you, and I'm thrilled to welcome you into the family. I only wish we could've been here for your wedding." Zack was impressed by how deftly the older woman put Tory at ease. His friend's wife had lived a hard life and rarely relaxed.

"We more or less eloped," Ben threw in.

"We should give them a proper reception, Carol. The old house could use some livening up."

"What a great idea!" Carol exclaimed. "We'll let you kids get settled back into school and then plan something." She looked beyond the adults to the empty room behind them. "Is little Alex here?" she asked wistfully. "It's been so long since we had a child in the family."

"She's in the bedroom playing a video game she got for Christmas," Tory answered. "I'll go get her."

As Tory left the room, Zack took the opportunity to excuse himself. Ben had been without family virtually his entire life. He deserved these moments alone with the couple who seemed completely ready to become the parents he'd never had.

There were times when life actually turned out right.

SHE COULDN'T GO. Someone would have to call him and tell him she wasn't going.

Randi paced from her closet to the full-length mirror in her bathroom, looking at herself in her standard gym shorts and T-shirt, her white socks and tennis shoes. She wasn't date material. She was too strong, too aggressive.

She didn't know how to be sweet and gushy and girlish.

She couldn't go.

She'd barely slept the night before, tossing and turning. She couldn't relax, couldn't get Zack Foster off her mind. He'd caused sensations in her that she didn't recognize. Had made her think about things she didn't usually bother with. Sex, for instance.

She'd never obsessed about a man in her life.

And when she *had* drifted off, she'd had a horrible dream about sitting in a restaurant, being herself, enjoying herself, and glancing up to see a look of revulsion on Zack Foster's face. Which alternated with indifference.

She couldn't go.

Her hair was okay. She had to keep it short so it didn't get in the way, but there was style to it. Bounce and casual curl. And the streaks of light blond mixed in with the darker blond were all natural. Her eyes were probably her best feature. Chocolate-brown—they were her older brother Will's eyes. She was proud to have them.

With one last look at herself, Randi turned her back on her reflection and grabbed the phone from the nightstand in her bedroom.

"Becca?" she said as soon as her sister-in-law picked up the phone.

"Randi, I just called you, but you didn't answer."

"I'm not at school."

"Where are you?" Will's wife asked. "Is everything okay?"

"Everything's fine," Randi said automatically. Then she remembered the day, almost a year before, when Becca had shown up on her doorstep, desperate, unsure, frightened. Of everyone she knew in Shelter Valley, she'd come to Randi.

"Well… I'm home, not sick or anything, but I'm not exactly fine," she clarified.

"What's up?"

"First, you have to promise me that you won't say anything to Will. Or anyone else, for that matter."

"You know you can trust me."

She did know that. Which was one reason she was on the phone at all. Becca was the epitome of discretion. It was Becca's mother, Rose, who was the town gossip.

Of course, Rose was harmless, since much of her gossip bore only a minute resemblance to the truth, and everyone knew that.

"I've got a date tonight."

"You do?" Becca couldn't quite keep the excitement out of her voice, but Randi gave her full marks for effort.

"Yeah."

"Okay, you have my permission to go. Just be home by midnight."

"It's with Zack Foster. He's the new partner Cassie took on at the clinic last spring."

"Oh?"

Randi almost smiled at the eagerness Becca was trying hard to conceal. Except that she felt so miserable smiling wasn't currently an option.

"I can't go," she muttered.

"Why not?" There was curiosity and concern in Becca's tone, though no condemnation.

Randi relaxed enough to sit down on the side of her bed.

"I don't know, Bec," she admitted. "I've only met the man once and he...he scares me."

"Zack? I've seen him a couple of times and he's big, I'll grant you. But a teddy bear. Besides, since when have you ever let a man frighten you? I can remember when you were barely five years old and challenging your teenage brothers, fully believing you could take them on."

"I could." She did smile this time.

"Yeah, because you had them wrapped around your sweet little finger."

"I could still take them on," Randi asserted. She had learned a long time ago that the mind was a far more effective weapon than physical strength. When she'd been on the professional golf tour, before the accident that had squelched that particular dream, it hadn't been the strength of her swing that had made her a winner. It had been the mental control and finesse that went along with her swing.

"It's not that Zack scares me, exactly," she said now to Becca, staring down at the logo on her shoe. "When I was sitting in his office yesterday, it was almost like I'd been hypnotized. I was practically ready to agree to whatever he said. It was the oddest sensation."

"You like him."

"I like you, too, but I don't lose my ability to think when I'm with you."

CHAPTER FOUR

"THAT'S DIFFERENT. I'm a woman."

"Yeah?" Randi replied. "No kidding."

Becca ignored her sarcasm. "Did your stomach flutter, too?" she asked knowingly.

"Yeah," Randi answered a little more slowly. The logo on her shoe was dirty. Dirty shoes always bothered her. "But that might've been because I skipped breakfast." She carried the phone with her as she went into the bathroom to take a wet washcloth to her shoe.

"And you couldn't stop looking at him?"

"Maybe." The smudge wouldn't come off. Damn.

"You've got the hots for him."

That was precisely what scared Randi. She didn't know *how* to have the hots. And she was a little old to be finding out.

"I've been attracted to a man before." She told Becca the same thing she'd told herself at least a hundred times since she'd awoken that morning.

"You're speaking of Sean?"

"Yes, mainly."

"Sweetie, you didn't give a damn if you were with

Sean or not. You went out with him for so long because it was convenient."

"I wouldn't sleep with a man without feeling *something* for him," Randi defended herself, walking to her closet for another pair of athletic shoes.

"I'm not saying you weren't fond of him, but there was no spark between the two of you. Will and I saw that right off the bat."

Which might explain why sex with Sean had been so terrible she'd only tried it with him twice. Once he'd made the initial move to her bedroom, she'd had to initiate everything else. And had found the experience more embarrassing than arousing.

Grabbing one of the nine other pairs of athletic shoes lined up in front of her, she slipped out of the ones she had on and put them aside for bleaching.

"Do you think there's something wrong with me?" Randi whispered. She didn't usually allow herself to think that way, but sometimes, in the dark of the night, she was unable to keep her fears at bay.

"No!" Becca's answer was emphatic. "You've just led an unusual life. You were an athlete from the day you were born. What choice did you have with four older brothers? You had to join in or be left in the dust. And you were good at everything you tried. You started training before you got to high school, and when most girls were experimenting with their sexuality, with boys, you were traveling on the junior professional golf circuit. You were hardly home enough to be able to graduate from high school, let alone do any dating.''

All of what her sister-in-law was saying Randi had already told herself. But it sounded so much more reasonable coming from Becca.

''And by the time I'd reached my twentieth birthday, I was on the LPGA tour and most men were too intimidated by me to see me as a woman. I usually knew more about sports than they did, and if a man happened to know as much, it was because he was an athlete himself, and then the fact that I might be able to beat him at his own game became a problem.''

''Tanner Snow?'' Becca named the golfer Randi had brought home for Christmas one year.

Randi tied the laces on the shoe she'd just put on. ''Yeah.''

''And it hasn't gotten any easier, has it, since you won the position at Montford?''

''Probably not.'' Randi hadn't really noticed. Had she? She liked her life. Had more friends than she knew what to do with, enjoyed the time she spent with them.

Not everyone had a strong sex drive—which was surely why she hadn't had a better experience with Sean.

Randi expended her physical energy on the basketball and tennis courts. And occasionally on the golf course, when she could bring herself to play a round with a rotator cuff that would never be what it was, thanks to the car accident nine years ago.

"Will and I have always said that when you got hit, you'd get hit hard," Becca said.

"Got hit?" She studied the logos on her shoes. They were clearly legible.

"Fell for a man."

"I've just met him, Becca! I haven't fallen anywhere."

"Have it your way." Randi couldn't tell if her brother's wife was humoring her or not.

"So will you call him and tell him I can't go? Say I have the flu or something?" She lay back on the end of her bed, staring at the ceiling.

"Why can't you call him?"

"Because I might do something stupid, like let him talk me into going."

"And that would be so horrible?"

"I think so."

"Why?"

Randi swallowed. "Because it *matters*." The admission was hard. "I don't know why. I can't understand it. But it matters."

"So how will not going to dinner with him help that?"

"I won't have to sit there and know things aren't going to work out." Randi sat up and bounced her feet on the floor.

"*How* do you know it won't?"

"It never does."

"There's a first time for everything."

Yesterday was certainly a case in point. "He's a total pet freak."

"He's a vet."

"I hate pets."

"You've never had one."

"I'm trying to sabotage the pet-therapy club assignment."

"How are you going to do that?" Becca asked, chuckling.

"I don't know." Randi planted her feet solidly on the floor. "Plan A was yesterday and something went drastically wrong. I haven't figured out Plan B yet, but rest assured, I will."

"Go to dinner and maybe it'll come to you."

She'd never thought of that. Dinner would be an excellent opportunity to talk Zack Foster out of using college students for his little service project this semester. She had to get this settled before the students were back in session the following week; this might be her last opportunity.

And when Zack saw the benefits to his schedule, he'd be thanking her for it.

"Do you realize what time it is?"

Zack looked at his watch. Holy hell, somehow it had jumped from eight-thirty to almost midnight without his even noticing. "I'm sorry," he said, signaling for their bill. "You probably have to work in the morning, don't you?"

Randi shrugged. Her shoulders, snug in the tight spandex jumpsuit she was wearing, attracted his attention. Everything about Randi's body was tight.

It made Zack tight, too.

"Classes don't start until next week, so while I have to go in, it doesn't have to be too early."

He had a surgery scheduled at seven-thirty the next morning.

"This place was great," Randi said, pushing through the front door of the five-star Scottsdale hotel he'd chosen—before she remembered that he would probably have opened it for her. "You were right—not only was the duck à l'orange superb, but that guitar player was fabulous."

He hadn't heard much of the music. He'd been too focused on hearing about Randi's job as athletic director at a class-one university. He'd learned the inside scoop on recruiting and eligibility rules, about Title Nine's effect on the world of sports and found out which sports brought in money at the gate. He'd guessed right on basketball, but missed volleyball by a long shot. He'd told Randi about his job, too, when she'd asked. For someone who had no fondness for pets, she certainly had a lot of questions.

And a load of sassy comebacks, too. Zack couldn't remember when he'd laughed so hard. Or just plain enjoyed himself so much.

What they hadn't talked about was the pet-therapy club.

"So did you go immediately to Montford after you

graduated from high school?'' he asked Randi as he reluctantly turned his Explorer back toward Shelter Valley. Despite the lateness of the hour, he wasn't ready for the evening to end.

Randi shook her head. Her blond hair reminded him of Meg Ryan's in that movie *French Kiss*—all flyaway and sexy as hell.

''Actually, I wasn't planning to attend college at all.''

He turned to look at her. ''You're kidding, right? Your brother's president of the local university.''

''When I graduated from high school, I was already turning pro. There was hardly time to think about more education. Besides, I thought I had all the education I needed in order to get where I was going.''

Something prickled the back of his neck. ''Turning pro?''

She grinned at him. ''I forget you're relatively new to town. Nobody talks about it much anymore, probably out of kindness to me, but you're riding with Shelter Valley's ex–child star of the Ladies Professional Golf Association.''

Tension shot through him. ''Golf?''

''Yeah.'' She nodded slowly, looking straight ahead at the dark road. ''I was good at a lot of sports, but my first love was golf. I was competing—and winning—by the time I was fourteen. By twenty, I was officially on the LPGA tour and slated to break all the records.''

Golf. He swallowed. Adjusted his big frame in the seat. Did that mean she knew Barbara Sharp? Did she know Dawn, too?

"What happened?"

"I was in a car accident in Florida not quite ten years ago. On my way to play the final round in a tournament with a purse of one hundred grand. I was up by five strokes going into the day and some idiot ran a red light and broadsided me two blocks from the golf course."

Golf. But almost ten years ago. Then she wouldn't know Dawn. And maybe not Barbara, either.

"You were driving?"

"Nah, I was in a cab. The back passenger door took the brunt of the collision and I was on the other side of that door. My right rotator cuff was crushed. And so was any future I'd hoped to have swinging a golf club."

"I'm sorry." He responded to the pain in her voice. And to the sick feeling he had in his own gut. She'd been a golfer.

"You seem so cheerful," he told her, "like nothing really bad ever came your way."

Turning to face him as much as she could within the confines of her seat belt, Randi took a moment to answer him. Already he knew that meant she was going to be completely serious. Randi had a tendency to blurt out the first thing that came to her mind. And it was often tempered with a large dose of her dry wit.

"The way I choose to see things, I'm very lucky," she finally said. There was no doubting that she meant every word. "I have a great family—the best. A job I love, a job many women spend their entire lives aiming for but never get. And I had a chance to live a dream, too. That's more than most people have. Life on the circuit is tough. Lonely. Still, I would've loved every minute of that life... But I love Shelter Valley, too."

"So you don't miss golf? Or get frustrated because you can't play?" Was the woman superhuman?

"Are you crazy? Of course I do," she said. "Just last week I went into Phoenix to play some rounds with a couple of friends. They're still on the circuit and wanted me to critique some problems they were having. By the last round, I was in tears. But I played until the bitter end."

Zack glanced at her. "Your shoulder hurt?"

"Yeah, but not enough to make me cry."

Not wanting to impinge on her privacy, Zack didn't ask any more. But he waited, hoping she'd tell him, anyway.

And wondered if the people she'd been playing with knew Barbara Sharp.

"I just got so tired of my head telling my body what to do—and my body not doing what it was told. My game was mediocre at best."

"Why play, then?" he asked, but he knew the answer. Probably the same reason he still played basketball even after he'd been cut from the college team his senior year. Some was better than none.

"Because I love the game. I love being on the course, smelling the fresh-cut grass, the feel of the club in my hands, the slight sting as the club makes contact with the ball. I love the sound of the ball falling into the cup. I'm still pretty damn good at putting."

"You could always take up miniature golf," he offered, throwing her a grin.

"Yeah, but those fake greens..."

They drove in silence for a couple of minutes. Disappointment and warnings rang in his head. He'd had a great time tonight. Far better than he'd expected. But that was all. He couldn't read more into it than a very pleasant evening.

Zack didn't do long-term relationships. Not anymore. Short and sweet had become his motto. Long enough for pleasure on both sides. Not long enough for either party to become disenchanted.

And he sure as hell wasn't ready to take up with a golfer. Even if she'd been out of the game for ten years. A man could only stand so much.

"But she's a woman." His own words rang silently in his ears as he recalled the pathetic happiness he'd seen in his wife's eyes.

He wanted to ask Randi if she knew Barbara, a woman he'd never met. But the words stuck in his throat. Because he didn't want to know or because he did? He wasn't sure. He just knew he didn't want to think about that part of his life. It was over.

THE FIRST WEEK of school came and went before Randi had a chance to stop long enough to acknowledge it. And she didn't even have any classes to teach. A couple of regional conference meetings, budget requests from disgruntled coaches and the hiring of new game-management personnel were only a few of the tasks that occupied her time.

In spite of its small size, Montford, with its dormitories and full scholarships, was a Division One school. In many respects, this was good. From Randi's perspective, it meant a lot of extra pressure. Pressure to find the best of the best if she was going to direct winning teams and keep her job.

Having grown up in the world of competitive sports, Randi was not afraid of pressure. She actually thrived on it. But it helped when she could focus one hundred percent of her energies on the task at hand.

She wasn't focusing that week. Hadn't focused since Zack Foster had dropped her off at her door without so much as a peck on the cheek a week and a half earlier. Things had been going so well, too. Right up until the part where she'd mentioned her previous pro status.

And why should that surprise me?

Disgruntled, knowing she had to be energetic when she showed her face at the women's tennis match later that afternoon, Randi gave in to her need for comfort and picked up the phone.

"Hey, it's Randi," she said as soon as she recognized the voice on the other end of the phone.

"What's up, woman? Got another revelation for me? Another good tip to help me improve my swing?"

"No." Randi grinned. Barbara was slated for the number-one spot on the LPGA tour this year, in spite of all the younger athletes coming up behind her.

"I was planning to send you flowers or something, to thank you again for all your help a couple of weeks ago, but I know you hate to see them die."

"Putting me up at the Phoenician and feeding me for three days wasn't payment enough?" Randi asked. Barbara was one of the two friends she'd spent time with the week before school started. On the golf course, using her sharp eye and years' worth of studying every intricate detail of the game, she'd critiqued their performances. And wept with frustration as she watched others do what she could no longer do herself.

Barbara had been the only one who'd seen her tears on the back nine that last day.

"The hotel was comped, and you know it," Barbara said. "And seriously, Ran, I really appreciate your help. You hit that slight weight switch perfectly. I haven't been able to miss since we straightened that out."

Randi fidgeted with a pencil on her desk. "Glad I could help."

"So what *can* I do to return the favor?"

"Remind me *why* we care about the things we care about."

"This sounds serious."

"Have you ever regretted what you gave up to be who you are?" Randi asked before she realized how stupid the question sounded. Barbara was at the top of her career, making more money than Randi had seen in years. Kind of hard to regret.

"Yeah."

Randi dropped the pencil, leaning back in her chair with one foot propped on the desk in front of her. "Yeah?"

"There are downsides to everything."

Of course there were. For every mountain climbed, a valley lay on the other side. Randi knew that, counseled her young athletes with such truths at every banquet she attended, every speech she gave. Without the bad, how could one measure the good? With no losers, there could be no winners.

But...

"So what do you regret most?"

"Same thing you do, I imagine," Barbara said, her no-nonsense voice tinged with the warmth she reserved only for those she considered real friends. "The circuit, the training, the life of a professional athlete, particularly a female professional athlete, exacts its price. You have to have complete focus, keep your mind and heart on one goal—to be the best. And suddenly you aren't a kid anymore with your whole life stretching before you.''

Her fingers straightening the lace on her tennis shoe, Randi froze.

''You wake up one morning and find yourself all alone in a world of couples,'' Barbara continued.

Or you lie awake one night, alone in a bed big enough for two, on a street lined with houses filled with families. In a town of moms and dads and people pulling together.

''And you discover,'' Randi said slowly, ''that not only are you alone, you don't have the slightest idea how to change that.''

''Wonder why nobody told us when we were growing up that while we were building one kind of skill, we were missing out on another. All the emotional stuff—the dates, the fumbling first kisses, the hurt feelings. Those were experiences we needed and didn't get.''

''They didn't tell us any of that stuff because winning is everything,'' Randi told her friend, the knowledge as natural to her as the air she breathed. Competition was a fact of life, and the point of competing was to win.

''We just didn't know, until it was too late, that when we chose to win physically, we were losing something else just as vital,'' Barbara murmured.

''But it's not necessarily fatal,'' Randi said now, barely hiding the question in her statement.

Barbara had managed, somehow, to win on all counts. She and Randi never spoke of the relationship Barbara had embarked on almost a year before. Randi had never even met the woman, but she knew the relationship was stronger than ever.

She'd seen the change in her friend. The easy light in her eyes, the peace that had replaced the nervous tension in Barbara's every movement.

"It's damn hard," Barbara said slowly, "to coax out that emotionally retarded child inside of you. To risk feeling like a fool as you learn things about yourself, about life, that most people learn when they're teenagers."

Randi wasn't sure she wanted to hear this. And yet, wasn't it exactly why she'd called her friend? Because she knew Barbara had grown up the same way she had—with one hundred percent dedication to her goals.

And they were women in a man's world, to boot. Fighting not only to develop their talents to almost impossible levels, they'd also had to compete with men—for sponsorships, for trainers, for facility time. Even for comps. All the factors essential to a young athlete's success came so much more readily to men than to women.

She and Barbara and others like them had had to be strong on every front. Which left no room whatsoever for the softer things in life. Like giving one's heart.

Yet Barbara had finally found a way. She'd come

to terms with her sexuality. She'd risked everything for the chance to not be alone.

"And what if you're more comfortable with the status quo?" Randi asked.

"Of course you're more comfortable," Barbara said. "Who wouldn't be? It's what you're familiar with, what you know."

"And you think that's wrong?"

"Not necessarily. Not if comfortable is enough for you."

"And if it isn't?" Randi wasn't sure one way or the other; she just wanted to be aware of all the possibilities.

"Then you have a long—uncomfortable—road ahead of you."

CHAPTER FIVE

THE FOLLOWING MONDAY, almost two weeks after her not-quite-successful date with Zack Foster, the Montford Pet Therapy Club held its first meeting. Several creative excuses for missing the get-together entertained Randi on and off throughout that day.

Maybe her Jeep was in the shop and if she didn't pick it up by four o'clock, she couldn't have it until the next day and then she'd have no way to get to work in the morning. Or to escape her home that evening in case of some dire emergency.

She worked on that one for quite a while, coming up with different angles, but eventually dismissed it. Her Jeep was brand-new, for one thing; she had no intention of depriving herself of its use, for another— even if that meant she had to see Zack Foster again.

She'd have claimed a sick dog or cat or fish she had to rush home to, except the reason that wouldn't work was obvious. If she was going to make a fool of herself with an asinine excuse, it had to at least be one that would fly.

The sick-grandmother thing was overused. Emergency baby-sitting might be good if there weren't about a thousand substitutes for her services in this town full of college students.

She had cramps.

That might be true, but absolutely none of Zack Foster's business.

She was allergic to animals? But then why hadn't she mentioned that from the outset? And wasn't that something her brother would've known before assigning her this ridiculous advisorship to begin with?

Still trying to come up with something at the last second, Randi locked her office early and headed toward the room in the student center that was to be the location of the dreaded meeting.

Why in hell couldn't there have been a tennis match that afternoon? Or a track meet? Or anything else that could even remotely pass as something that required her professional attention? Where were all the millions of things that took up every spare second of Randi's time on any other day?

Ten students were waiting in the room when Randi arrived. Ten students oohing and ahhing and making friends with the two canines drooling on the gray-tiled floor. Ten students, two drooling canines—and Zack Foster.

He looked as good as Randi remembered. Damn him. And damn *her* for noticing that, instead of inventing a plausible excuse.

"You're late," the man said when he noticed her hovering at the back of the room.

Only ten minutes. That wasn't bad.

"I know."

His eyes locked on her briefly and he looked as though he had more to say.

Randi just stood there.

"Meet Sammie and Bear," he finally said, indicating the furry masses holding court at his feet.

Glancing at them and then away, Randi turned to the students, instead.

"Okay, gang, let's all have a seat and figure out who we've got and what we're doing."

One of the first things she'd learned in life was to pretend she was always in control—even when she'd never felt *less* in control. Especially then.

SHE HADN'T GOTTEN any worse-looking in the two weeks since he'd seen her, Zack thought as he leashed Sammie and Bear and stood waiting while Randi got the meeting under way. If anything, she looked even more desirable than he'd remembered. With her cropped blond hair, that narrow waist and those firm legs that went on forever outside those indecently tight shorts she'd worn two out of the three times he'd seen her—didn't the university pay her enough to afford longer pants?—she'd cause any red-blooded guy to take a second look.

There was nothing wrong with looking.

"So, if you're all comfortable with the time commitment, I need to have you sign here, leave me a phone number and, if you're living on campus, your dorm. If you're off campus, put your address here…''

She turned the clipboard she was holding so they could all see the various lines on the form and then passed it, and a pen, to the young man closest to her.

Damn, but she made running shoes seem sexy. Something about the way she moved in them…

Leaning down to Sammie and Bear, one hand on each of them as he scratched behind their ears, Zack shook his head to free himself from distracting thoughts. He was there to do a job. A worthy and necessary job to which he was honestly dedicated.

Finding running shoes sexy was kind of sick.

Sammie licked his cheek just as Zack saw Randi look in his direction, her upper lip curled slightly in distaste. She resumed talking to the students.

"In just a moment I'll be turning the meeting over to Dr. Zack Foster. He's a veterinarian here in Shelter Valley. He and his partner are establishing pet-therapy programs similar to this one in universities all over the country, apparently with a great deal of success. I'm sure he'll tell you some of the stories.…''

At least she'd done her homework. Zack was impressed.

He only had to see her on five occasions throughout the semester. And he'd have animals with him every time. He'd be safe.

"Ms. Parsons is right," Zack began when the floor was his. "My partner, Dr. Cassie Tate, and I have been visiting universities throughout the country. But I'm in charge of this portion of our pet-therapy program.''

Although he refused to actually look at her, he followed Randi's progress as she moved to the back of the room and perched on one of the desks. Sammie sat beside him, watching the students as though she was in the know. Bear lay down under a desk, his head on his paws.

''Dr. Tate is involved in a very serious aspect of our work. In partnership with psychiatrists across the country, she works on problems with a much bigger scope than we'll encounter. She and her specially trained animals deal with patients who have emotional disorders and mental illnesses—people who are clinically depressed, bipolar, that type of thing.''

In spite of himself, he glanced up at his partner in this particular venture, wondering if she'd revised her assumption yet that they were all wasting their time in believing animals could help in the treatment of real human distress.

She was studying her shoes, tapping them silently on the chair in front of her. At least she wasn't asleep. There was a chance she was listening.

Not that her opinion of his work mattered at all.

He and Cassie had met opposition on more than one occasion, but opposition didn't intimidate him in the slightest. The success of their work spoke for itself.

He returned his attention to the eager faces before

him. "We'll be working strictly with the elderly," he told them, briefly describing the different homes they'd visit.

Sammie stood, realized she was still on her leash and sat down again.

"Are we going to be working with these dogs?" One of the girls, a short slightly heavy girl with long dark hair, asked.

Zack nodded. "These and others. Sammie's been a therapist for almost three years now."

The dog, hearing her name, turned in a circle and barked, her leash getting tangled around one front paw.

Laughter erupted, and Sammie, as if sensing the interest directed at her, barked again.

Randi was still studying her shoes.

"What does he do?" A long-haired young man asked curiously, pointing at Bear.

"Gives people someone to identify with," Zack said with a smile, although he was absolutely serious. "He shows them how to grow old without fear."

A couple of girls in the front row nodded.

"You'll be working in pairs," Zack continued. "We'll have a total of five dogs, one for each pair of you. The dogs have all been through obedience classes and rigorous health screenings. They're all veteran therapists."

"Do we get training, too?" A young man with a blond crewcut asked.

Zack shook his head, looking up as his peripheral

vision caught movement in the back of the class-room. Randi was doing some kind of stretching thing, her right arm bent and pulled behind her head, her left hand grasping the elbow and pushing it far-ther.

Her breasts, as firm as everything else about her, were thrown into prominence, garnering a reaction from Zack that he didn't appreciate. Dammit, why couldn't the woman just pay attention?

"Uh, no," he said slowly, forcing himself to focus on the job at hand. "You're basically escorts. You take the animals into the predetermined rooms and then stand back while the animals do their jobs. There may be times when you need to participate, perhaps talk to the patients, but that would entail no more than casual conversation."

Randi was looking down again, studying her knee-caps, as far as Zack could tell. He felt a twinge of envy that she could study those legs any time she pleased.

"One visit last semester, we had a woman who refused to take her pills. She wouldn't let any one of the staff near her. After half an hour with Sammie, she'd relaxed enough to let Sammie's escort hand her the pills and a cup of water and she took every one of them without complaint."

"Cool." The long-haired fellow nodded his head.

"These dogs do a lot of cool things," Zack said. "Scientific studies have proved that petting a dog can lower blood pressure. Dogs have been successfully used to alleviate depression. Pets have even been shown to lengthen the life span of their owners.

"For our patients, they often provide comfort and companionship in days that are otherwise relentlessly the same."

At the back of the room, there was movement again. Randi was now sitting on her hands, and her attention seemed to be moving up. Her gaze was set on the back of the heavy girl's head.

"We've also had success with patients who are struggling with memory deficiencies. In several cases, an individual hasn't remembered a dog's escort or his own caregivers' names, but he's always remembered the dog's name."

After another fifteen minutes, Zack wrapped up his introduction and turned the meeting back to Randi to schedule the dates of their visits. These kids all seemed eager, receptive. But then, they usually were at Montford.

He'd call the nursing homes in the morning to let them know when they'd be coming. And he'd check on the other dogs' availability, as well. Sammie and Bear were a given, but the other dogs he used had owners whose schedules he had to accommodate.

They were going to have a great semester.

"If we can't fit in all five visits…"

Amend that. They were going to have a great semester—maybe.

Zack stepped forward, Sammie stood, turned two circles and barked.

"We're completely open on the dates," he said, "subject to your availability and that of the dogs. Weekdays, weekends, evenings. That's the thing about old folks in nursing homes. They're pretty much always there."

Looking annoyed, Randi nodded. "So, I know you all have busy schedules. Some of you are graduating in May. Most of you will have projects and other activities that take up your time." She paused to let that sink in while Zack bored a hole in her head with his eyes.

He'd love to get his hands on that sleek neck of hers.

Actually, he'd like to get his hands *anywhere* on that body of hers....

"So, how many of you think you'll actually be able to handle five visits?"

Zack was happy to note a unanimous show of hands.

"Or we could try for three or four," Randi said.

Could the woman not count?

"No, five's good," someone said.

"Five's not a problem."

"I'd like to do more than five. Could we talk about that?" another student asked.

"Five it is, then," Randi interrupted quickly. She stared down at her leather-bound day planner. Mesmerized by the pulse beating in her neck, Zack listened while the dates were agreed upon. He didn't smile. Not once.

At least not so anyone could see.

As each date was confirmed, she fidgeted a little more. A finger tapping the page of her planner. One foot tapping silently on the floor. Finally she began chewing on her lower lip in a way that Zack found rather disconcerting.

He no longer felt like smiling.

"YOU BUSY?"

Randi looked up from the scouting report she was reading in her office to see Zack Foster standing there.

The very person she'd been trying to avoid thinking about. She certainly didn't want to see him. Especially in her private sanctum. The room was too small for both of them.

"You left the meeting last night before I had a chance to give you these," he said, setting some pamphlets and a book on the corner of her paper-littered desk.

"You were surrounded by admirers," she said, trying not to notice how firm his pecs looked in the polo shirt he was wearing. Didn't the man know it was winter outside?

So what if it was supposed to hit the mid-seventies all week? He could still acknowledge the season with a long-sleeved shirt. Or even a coat. Something big and bulky that would leave everything to the imagination.

Or would it?

She glanced down at the stuff he'd brought.

If she had to guess, she'd say a coat wouldn't do a damn thing to hide the man's impressive physique.

Not that she *was* guessing.

"What are these?" she asked, pretending to take an interest in the pamphlets. They had pictures of dogs on the front.

Boring.

How could she be reacting so strongly to a man who spent his whole life thinking about something that bored her to tears? His obsession with animals was worse than her youngest brother's obsession with cars.

"They're a pet-therapy crash-training course for you," Zack answered her. He commanded the space around him as though the office was his, not hers. "It was obvious last night that you'd done your homework on Cassie and me, and on what we do. Now it's time to learn a little more about pet therapy generally."

"You said last night the kids don't need training."

"They don't. You do."

"Why?" she demanded. She wasn't going to be handling any pets. She was merely supervising— along for the ride.

"How can you be an adviser for something you don't understand?" he asked, gazing at her narrowly.

Her stomach quivered.

"What's to understand?" she muttered.

"My point exactly," Zack said, flicking the edge

of the pamphlet she held. "You'll find the answer to that question right there."

Randi wasn't used to failure. Didn't like it a bit. And she'd failed utterly to convince him that he should call the whole thing off.

"You sure you aren't too busy to do this?" She shot him an engaging grin that almost always worked on Will.

"Positive."

So much for the grin. Randi shifted, put her feet up on her desk. And then, noticing his appreciative look at the long bare expanse of leg, dropped them again.

"Why is this so important to you?" she asked, frustrated.

He shrugged those impressive shoulders. "Why are sports important to you?"

She opened her mouth, ready with a smart reply. And then closed it again, frowning.

Somehow, in her view, handling a dog just didn't compare with handling a golf club—or even a basketball.

"Sports give people—a huge percentage of the population—pleasure."

"So do pets." He crossed his arms.

Randi leaned back in her chair, determined to meet the challenge she'd just been thrown.

"Okay, but sports provide our economy with a huge chunk of revenue."

"Ditto."

"How do you figure?" She sat forward, forearms on her desk. "Season tickets to one sports event are surely more than the cost of a dog. And how often does someone buy a dog? Every fifteen years?"

"Buying a pet is the least of the expenses. There are vet's bills—"

"Surely you aren't charging your patients several hundred dollars for vaccinations!"

His brow creased. "I do far more than just give vaccinations."

Okay, so that had been a cheap shot. "But most people aren't spending hundreds of dollars a year on animal surgeries, are they?"

"No, but they do, easily, on pet food."

Oh, right. Food.

He was meeting her point for point with a straight face, but his sharp blue eyes sparkled with challenge. "And then there are pet supplies," he continued. "That's a billion-dollar industry."

"Just like we have uniforms and shoes," she said, nodding. "Yeah, I can see that."

"And trainers," he added with a grin.

Her stomach flopping again, Randi slumped back in her chair. "How did we get started on this ridiculous conversation, anyway?"

"You were wondering about the economic importance of what I do. And I think we were just getting to the part where you were going to have to admit defeat."

She stood up. He sounded just a bit too pleased with himself.

"I'll make you a deal," she said suddenly, half-desperate.

He cocked his head, the crease back between his brows. "What kind of deal?"

"You meet me on the basketball court in five minutes. We play ten minutes of one-on-one. I win, no pet therapy this semester."

"And if you don't win, you'll take on the club wholeheartedly and participate willingly?"

She paused, trying to imagine herself ever willingly getting close enough to a dog to be its partner, and then shook her head. She wasn't going to lose. Randi was almost as good at basketball as she'd been at golf. Rotator cuffs weren't essential to basketball the way they were to golf.

"Okay," she finally said.

"I'm not dressed for the court." He looked down at his jeans.

Her gaze followed his. And she took a shaky breath.

"You're wearing running shoes," she said.

"You're wearing gym shorts."

"You're taller than I am by a foot, which more than makes up for the shorts advantage."

"Ten minutes, huh?" he asked, studying her.

"I'll set the clock."

"You're on."

Her heart began to pound. "You're serious?" She

was finally going to get somewhere? Get him and his pet-therapy club off her back? Out of her life?

Because surely, when she demonstrated her prowess on the court, showed him that she could defeat him, the appreciation she saw in his eyes would fade—just as it had when she'd told him about her time with the LPGA.

If there was one fact Randi had learned growing up with four brothers, it was that the male ego was a fragile thing. And there were some blows it couldn't take.

Unable to completely ignore her conscience, Randi said, "I have to warn you, I'm pretty good."

"Trying to get out of it already?" he asked. "What's the matter, afraid you can't beat me?"

"On the contrary." She pinned him with the gaze that had been intimidating opponents all her life. "I *know* I can."

He wasn't fazed. "Then lead the way."

He stood back, waiting for her to pass him. Meeting his glance, Randi did. And held her breath until she was safely in front of him, away from the danger of his tantalizing male scent—and the compelling look in his eyes.

CHAPTER SIX

HE'D NEVER GOTTEN a hard-on during a basketball game before. Jumping up to sink a three-pointer that would give him a one-point lead, Zack braced himself for the pain of the landing. His jeans were squeezing the life out of him.

In all the years he'd been married to Dawn, he'd never hurt so bad.

Just as the ball sailed off his fingertips, Randi slammed into him, her hand catching the elbow of his shooting arm.

"That's a foul," he said, wincing as he landed back on the floor and his jeans pulled taut across his thighs.

"Nonshooting foul." Her ragged breathing, echoing in the deserted gym, sent another wave of heat through him.

She passed the ball to him, he went for a quick two, sank the ball, tied the game and stayed right with her as they chased to the other end of the court. They spent the next couple of minutes trading defensive moves that would have made the NBA proud.

It kept them from scoring baskets. It didn't help Zack's pain at all.

What was it with this woman? he wondered as he stole the ball from her. Sure she was great-looking, but so were most of the women he'd dated—before and after his marriage.

Never had a woman affected him the way this one did.

"My ball," she called when he reached in for another steal, making the steal, but fouling her, as well.

He bounced the ball to her with a little more energy than necessary.

She turned to head back up the court and he adjusted his jeans as he ran after her.

He caught her mid-court, reaching around her to grab the ball, and grazed her breast. He felt more than heard her rushed intake of breath. Good. She wasn't immune to the energy charging the room.

Though why it mattered, Zack wasn't sure. Unless maybe he had a score to settle. She was an ex-golfer. An athlete. There was something horribly satisfying about the thought of being able to turn her on. To make her burn.

As he hadn't been able to do with Dawn.

She got past him and sank a beautiful hook shot.

Zack glanced at the clock. Thirty seconds left and she was up by two. He didn't miss the grin on her flushed face as she paralleled him up the court, arms flailing.

"Give it up, Foster," she said, her voice cocky even in its breathlessness.

"Forget it," he grunted. Planting himself on the

court, he raised his arms—and the ball—over his head where she couldn't reach them. She jumped, knocking into him, but he was immovable.

This woman was not going to get the better of him.

It wasn't about pet therapy anymore. It wasn't even about basketball. It was about a man and a woman who had something to settle.

He sank the shot just before the clock rang out.

"It's a draw," Randi said, breathing heavily. She sounded so disappointed he almost felt sorry for her.

"You've got some pamphlets to read." They were standing in center court.

"You didn't win," she stated, her gaze penetrating.

Trying to regulate his breathing, to pretend he wasn't as winded as she was, Zack shook his head. "I didn't have to," he told her triumphantly. "The deal was that if you win, we call off pet therapy for the semester. And if—"

"You win, I participate willingly," she interrupted.

"Uh-uh." He couldn't resist the smile pulling at his lips. "And if you *don't* win, you participate willingly."

He waited while she thought back to what they'd said, and he knew the instant she realized he was right.

"How many pamphlets do I have to read?" she asked. He had to hand it to her. She took it on the chin.

"Just the four I gave you. And the book, too."

"Don't expect me to like your dogs." She stood, feet apart, facing him in the middle of the deserted court.

Zack had to forcibly restrain himself from yanking her into his arms.

"I won't," he assured her. Though he had a lot of faith in Sammie and Bear.

Right then, however, it wasn't his dogs he wanted her to like.

"I'll have them read in a couple of days," she said, her eyes still meeting his.

Zack's respect for her grew.

"Have dinner with me again, and we can go over things."

For the first time since she'd issued her challenge, her eyes dropped.

"My treat," he said, anxious to pin her down to another meeting—to a time when he could explore the effect he seemed to have on her.

"When?" She lifted her chin.

"Thursday at seven?"

"Fine."

Zack left her then, whistling as he made his way out to his Explorer. Feeling quite satisfied with the morning's events, he ignored the little voice inside him that warned of the dangerous effect she had on him, too.

He knew the score. He wasn't looking for long-term. He wasn't looking for anything but a mutual exchange of pleasure.

There was no danger here. She was an athlete. He'd never be stupid enough to fall for an athlete. All he had to do was think of Dawn.

And her lover.

He'd been living with a lesbian. Sleeping with her, making love to her, and he hadn't even known. Not only had he not suspected that Dawn wasn't completely satisfied with the physical side of their relationship, he'd honestly believed they'd had a good marriage, that they were a team, complementing each other, meant to be together. *He'd* had complete faith in forever. *She'd* had another lover.

He wasn't going to be stupid enough to fall for anyone again. Period.

HE TOOK HER into Phoenix, not to the same hotel, but to a restaurant that was equally nice. Randi wasn't sure whether he was purposely keeping their association hidden from the people back home in Shelter Valley or if he just wanted to take her to places nicer than Shelter Valley had to offer. But she was glad of the anonymity just the same.

Randi Parsons on a date would create quite a stir. Randi Parsons dating the most eligible bachelor in town would probably make the front page of Shelter Valley's weekly paper.

If the gossips found out this was her *second* date with the most eligible bachelor in town, the paper might even announce her engagement. Not that she really cared what the paper said, but...

"Rumor has it you and Cassie could end up together," she blurted over dessert Thursday night. Things were going entirely too well that evening, and she had to find some way to slow things down.

She wasn't interested in having her entire life disrupted by a potentially cataclysmic and definitely short-lived relationship. A fling, an affair, was all it would be, not that she wanted anything permanent. Her life was settled. Content. Or it would be as soon as spring break arrived and she got her white picket fence.

"Rumor being the old gossips in town?" he asked, grinning lazily at her across the candle-lit table.

She shrugged, taking a long sip of wine. "Probably."

Finishing off his crème brûlé, he pushed the bowl aside and sat back, his eyes serious as he met her gaze. "The only passion there's ever been between Cassie and me is a shared passion for the work we do."

You have no reason to feel relief here, Randi told herself.

On the contrary, she should be feeling sorry for Cassie. The woman deserved some happiness.

"Have you known her long?" Randi asked.

Considering how much he loved his work, Cassie would be a perfect soul mate. And she was gorgeous, too.

"We met in college," he said, pausing for a sip from the wineglass he held as he sat comfortably in his chair. "And we've kept in touch ever since. She's a good friend, but there's never been anything more than that, for either of us."

Randi couldn't believe that. She couldn't imagine there was a woman alive who'd be impervious to Zack's appeal.

"You sure about that?" she asked him, eyes half-lowered as she watched for his reaction.

"Absolutely. When I met Cassie, the doors to her heart were already firmly shut."

Randi nodded, understanding, but also truly sad for the woman she'd grown up with yet hardly knew. At one time, Cassie Tate had the perfect life. the oldest of four girls, she'd grown up in a close-knit family, had had lots of friends. And in the space of a day, or so it seemed, it was all over. Her marriage to the town heir, Sam Montford. And more. There'd been some story about a baby, but everything had been kept very quiet, which meant it must have really been bad if the Shelter Valley gossips had been convinced to hold their tongues.

Not that Randi knew for sure; she'd been away a lot then, on the LPGA tour…

It took her a second to realize that she and Zack were simply staring at each other. Neither saying a word.

But once she'd noticed, she got nervous and cast down her eyes.

"Did you read the stuff I left for you?" His question brought things back to safety again.

"Yes." Randi had read every word in the book and the brochures he'd given her. She'd read the stuff she'd printed off the Internet, too.

"And?"

If knowledge was all it took to supervise, she was ready. But if it was a case of being able to put that knowledge into action, she might never be ready.

Her opinion of dogs had been formed at a very early age. Dogs were unpredictable. And they could hurt you.

"There were some pretty impressive statistics," she murmured.

He didn't actually say *I told you so,* unless you counted the grin that tilted those lips she couldn't get out of her mind.

"Pet therapy is a rapidly growing discipline," she went on. "And I could even see how, in some instances, the animals might be able to succeed where modern medicine can't." She was shocked by how badly she wanted to please him.

"Then you're ready to go to work."

Wrong.

"I'm not working. I'm supervising."

"I have enough dogs lined up for you to take one."

He was going to be disappointed in her if she didn't at least make an effort here. But...

"I'd, uh, feel more comfortable if I were free to,

uh, walk around and, you know, supervise—at least the first time out.'' She'd sure stumbled through that one. Not quite her style.

But then not a lot about her association with Zack Foster was happening with her usual assured style.

She let out a breath she hadn't realized she was holding when he nodded. ''If any of your students runs into a problem, you'll want to be available to take over.''

Okay. Yeah. That was it.

She couldn't actually lie to him—having grown up in Shelter Valley and working at Montford, where values were everything—so Randi let her silence do the lying for her. And tried to ignore the guilt.

They finished their wine, talked about their families. He knew about her four brothers, of course, since he'd lived in Shelter Valley for almost a year. He'd heard about her parents, too, but he'd only seen them from a distance at one of her basketball games.

But she knew nothing about his father, the lawyer, or his mother, the homemaker. Was intrigued to hear that he was an only child. Something that wasn't common in Shelter Valley, where big families were the rule. His folks lived in Colorado.

''Do you get to see them often?'' Randi asked. As much as she liked to pretend her family was a pain in the ass, she'd hate to live permanently apart from any of them.

''I go there a couple of times a year,'' he said.

"And they've been here twice. I'm hoping to convince them to move here."

"Did you grow up in Colorado?"

He nodded.

"So what brought you here?"

"I won a partial basketball scholarship to Arizona State my freshman year."

She frowned. "I don't remember seeing you—"

"I was cut from the team before my senior year. Never really played much…"

He'd won a college basketball scholarship and here she'd been feeling sorry for him when she'd issued that challenge on Tuesday. If she hadn't gone into that little match with a stacked deck herself, she'd call him on his duplicity.

The bill was paid and finally there was no reason to linger. Randi stood, disappointed that the evening was at an end. She knew this night was a time out of time—it had no relevance to her real life—but she'd never enjoyed herself so much on a date. Not that she'd been on all that many. She'd just never felt so…so completely comfortable. As if she and Zack existed on the same little patch of solid ground in a scattered and shaky universe.

And yet, she'd never felt so completely uncomfortable either. Her nerves were more ragged than they'd ever been—even before the most important golf championship game she'd played in the LPGA.

They didn't improve when he took her hand on the way to his Explorer.

He opened her door and Randi's heart expanded another little bit. Not many people understood that being an athlete didn't mean she didn't want to be pampered like any other woman now and then. Although she hadn't really known that herself until he'd shown her how it felt...

How had *he* known?

Just outside of town, when they hit the dark desert highway that led home, he took her hand again. And kept on holding it. They didn't say much. Just sat there, watching the road, feeling the night.

And that was okay, too.

Their silence left time for awareness—of physical sensation and realms of *feeling* she'd never experienced before.

She couldn't speak for Zack, but her body had never been more aware of another's. It was as though the hand holding hers was connecting her to some unfamiliar network, sending heated messages through her veins.

Coded messages that her mind couldn't understand, but that her body was answering, anyway.

It meant nothing. She knew that. It was going nowhere. She knew that, too. A man like Zack would want a woman like his partner, Cassie. One who was the epitome of womanhood. Whose hair wasn't short and practical. Who dressed in the latest and most feminine styles. Who wore high heels and makeup.

A woman who could make herself pet a dog.

Except he didn't want Cassie.

But he'd want someone like her. Randi was sure of that.

"This is a great house," he said appreciatively as he pulled up in front of her place.

"It needs a picket fence," she said, because she couldn't say what she was really thinking. That she wished the evening didn't have to end. "But I'm getting one soon."

"Is someone here?" he asked, walking her to the door.

"No." Could he actually be hinting? But what about the last time they'd gone out? He'd been charming then, too. Until he'd brought her home. After that, he couldn't leave fast enough.

"The lights are on."

"Oh." So much for hints. "I'm not very good about turning them off."

"You forget sometimes?" he asked, his hand lightly touching the small of her back as they climbed her steps. "It happens to everyone."

"Not really," she felt compelled to tell him. "I pretty much never turn them off."

Lights seemed friendly to her—almost as though they gave the house life. She found it comforting to have them on. Not that she'd admit it to anyone. Ever.

"You must get a hell of an electric bill."

"Yeah, but I cut other places. Like groceries. Doesn't take much to feed one. I eat a lot of energy bars and cereal."

"I know what you mean."

They were at her front door. Randi took as long as she could locating her key, but that stretched out the time by only about ten seconds, since it was in the pocket of the short leather jacket she'd worn over her black denim jeans and peach sweater.

He'd worn Dockers and a cream-colored oxford shirt with the sleeves rolled up. She was only slightly underdressed.

"Would you like to come in?"

The words escaped before she could stop them.

"Sure."

She didn't know which surprised her more—that she'd actually asked or that he'd accepted.

She had no idea what to do with him once they were inside. He seemed to fill her small foyer and to spill over into the living room that was separated from the foyer by her sofa.

"Have a seat," she said, clasping her hands in front of her like some silly high-school freshman entertaining the football team's senior quarterback.

What was it Barbara had said about their retarded social development?

Rather than sitting, Zack wandered around her living room, stopping to peruse the various pictures of her family displayed around the room.

"Must have been something, growing up with four boys," he mused, smiling at a photo of her and her brothers, taken almost fifteen years before. They'd all been hiking the red-rock mountains near Sedona and were sweaty and exhausted—but victorious—as they grinned into the camera. Becca, who'd waited for them at the bottom, had taken the shot.

"It wasn't so bad," she said, smiling as she looked at the photo again. The memory it brought back was special—an experience she treasured. She'd been one of them that day. "I never have to worry about my car breaking down or hiring movers!"

He turned to look at her. "They weren't overprotective?"

"Of course they were," Randi said, still smiling. "I just ignored them."

"You're something, you know that?" His words were soft, caressing her, as he moved closer.

Randi stood there, hypnotized, waiting for him. He was going to touch her. She could read his intentions in the half-lowered smoky eyes that were holding hers.

His hands settled on her shoulders at the same time his lips covered hers. Taking possession of her senses.

Lost, in a world she'd never truly known, Randi gave herself up to his touch, to his warm lips, his avid kiss. Her body flamed, adrenaline flowing through her so quickly it left her breathless.

Or was it the mouth covering hers that was consuming her breath?

Zack's tongue slid between her lips, tasting her, testing her. In the past, she'd endured it and wondered what all the fuss was about; this time it made her joints lose their strength.

She'd have fallen if he hadn't been holding her. If he hadn't led her over to her couch, guiding them down without ever breaking contact with her lips.

"You are beautiful," he whispered hoarsely, kissing her neck, her collarbone, before reclaiming her swollen wanton mouth.

Randi would've told him how incredible he was, if she'd been able to form the words.

Her hands flew over his body, his expansive shoulders, his back, the thick blond hair that just touched the back of his collar. His face.

So different from hers, that face. A bit rough with a day's stubble. There was so much character there. From the masculine chiseled cheekbones to the lines around his eyes, Zack's face spoke of a man's life. A life lived.

Randi was enthralled.

"I've been wanting to do this since you first walked into my office," he murmured, smoothing the hair back from her face. "You're so soft. So hot."

He slid his hands over her cheeks, down her neck and past her shoulders, taking both her breasts at the same time. Arching her back, Randi strained against that touch, welcoming it.

"I've never met anyone like you," she whispered, raising her head for another of his mesmerizing kisses.

Accepting the invitation, Zack kissed her again—

long and hard—all the while caressing her breasts through the soft angora of her sweater. The friction of his large callused hands against the soft wool was making her wild with wanting.

Wanting him. Wanting more.

There were no thoughts of this being too soon. Of this being so completely unlike her. The feelings he evoked were too compelling, so natural and perfect—so breathtakingly beautiful—there was no chance to be practical.

No reason to be afraid.

She was feeling things she'd never felt before. Things she'd sometimes wondered if she'd ever feel. She was so damned relieved she almost started to cry. She wasn't frigid. Or sexless. Sean just hadn't been the man to make her burn.

"I want you." Zack's voice was rough with desire as he drew away only far enough to look at her, to meet her eyes.

Randi nodded. "I want you, too," she whispered.

Now. She wanted him right now, before something happened to make this incredible feeling go away. Before he figured out that she didn't have what it took to keep him coming back.

Before she remembered that comfortable was safe, that all she needed was a white picket fence.

Before he got turned off by her aggression, or intimidated by her abilities, her strength. Her independence.

The last thing Randi felt, as she slowly led Zack Foster to her bedroom, was independent. She'd never felt more helpless in her life.

Or more impatient…

CHAPTER SEVEN

SOMETHING NIGGLED at the far reaches of Zack's mind, but he was too deafened by the passion roaring through his blood to take heed. To listen.

He reached into his back pocket for his wallet, sliding out the condom he always kept there; he tossed it onto the end of the bed before tackling Randi down to the very same spot.

The woman in his arms was perfection. Her skin, so smooth and soft, covered the firm feminine muscles. Softness and strength—the combination robbed him of coherent thought. He had to have more, touch every inch of her, see every inch of her. Enter her.

But more than his own needs, what fueled Zack past the point of accountability was the need he was arousing in Randi. Never had a woman been so out of control for him, ripping open his shirt, digging her fingers into the hair on his chest, playing with his nipples, while he played with her lips. Her hips ground against his as he lay on top of her across her bed.

Her moans were tickling his lips, her eyes begging him....

It was the most honest expression of physical hunger he'd ever known.

"Slow down, honey," he whispered, "so I can make it good for you."

Her hips pressing up into his groin, squeezing his hardened penis, Randi half chuckled. "It's already better than it's ever been."

The words filled him, relieved his insecurities, spurred him on.

"Let's get these clothes off you," he said, burying his face in her neck as he lifted her sweater.

Her bra was off by the time the sweater hit the floor, and Randi's breasts were naked and available for him to see, to touch, to taste.

And taste them he did, kissing her, suckling her, driving her—driving himself—beyond the point of reason.

Her jeans slid away; his pants and shirt joined them as they explored each other, leaving wet kisses and urgent caresses over every inch of exposed skin.

When he delved into places not quite exposed, Randi let out a moan that tore all the way through him. He wanted the moment to last longer, to explore her far more completely than he'd done, but he climbed on top of her, instead, barely taking time to sheath himself before he plunged deep inside her.

He'd meant to take things nice and slow, to move with her, not on her, but her body was so slick and ready, her cries so intense, he found himself riding her like a teenager in heat. She met him thrust for thrust, her fingers splayed across his buttocks, showing him what she wanted.

Zack barely held on until he felt her pulsating around him before he slid over the edge, reveling in a release that was more powerful than anything he'd ever experienced.

Spent, he supported himself on his forearms and stared down at her, telling her without words what she'd just done to him.

The woman was incredible.

AN HOUR LATER, physically sated though not at all sleepy, Zack slipped quietly into his slacks. Then, leaving them unzipped so as not to make any more noise than necessary, he collected the rest of his belongings and tiptoed out of Randi's room.

He had a feeling he'd made a huge mistake, going to bed with Randi Parsons. Going to bed with *anyone* in this town where anonymity was impossible. Where there would always be a morning after.

Especially with Randi Parsons. She wasn't a love 'em and leave 'em type.

And love 'em and leave 'em was all Zack did.

He'd just never done it so foolishly. Or without making certain that the woman in question knew the score.

He had to work with her, for crying out loud.

She was Will Parsons's little sister.

She had four older brothers, all within walking distance.

Maybe one of them would shoot him and put him out of his misery.

RANDI LAY SILENTLY in bed, pretending to sleep as Zack gathered his things. She didn't move—didn't want to risk having to speak with him, or worse, hearing anything he might have to say—until she heard her front door click shut.

She gave him another couple of minutes to get to his Explorer and down the street. Then she jumped out of bed and pulled on a pair of old familiar sweatpants and a matching soft fleece-lined shirt.

Hugging her arms around her body, feeling the fabric's softness against her skin, grasping at comfort wherever she could find it, she trailed slowly through her house, looking for a note. She didn't expect to find one. Men who sneaked out in the middle of the night, who sneaked out right after the loving, didn't leave notes.

They didn't leave tracks.

They just left.

She'd expected more from Zack Foster.

Fool that she was.

RELIEF.

It wasn't what she'd expected to feel when she woke up the next morning and remembered what had happened—remembered how it ended.

But as she dressed in her usual shorts and a long-sleeved waist-length underwear top, as she tied her running shoes, making sure the laces were even and lying flat, she had the most overwhelming sense of relief.

She'd had her night of fun—of decadence. She'd slaked the strange desire that had been consuming her. And she'd risked nothing. Not her routine, her comfortable life. Not her heart.

From here on out, it was business as usual.

Zack Foster certainly wasn't going to be asking any more of her, not after leaving the way he had the night before.

They could put the entire episode behind them and get on with it.

And if she felt a twinge of regret for the friend she might have had in Zack, for the incredible *something* she'd glimpsed the previous night, she shrugged off those thoughts as she'd shrugged off the occasional losses she'd had on the LPGA circuit.

Life wasn't perfect.

But it was pretty damn close.

The first thing she did when she got to her office that morning was order herself a white picket fence, scheduled to be installed in March, during spring break.

"Randi, you got a minute?" Brad Bordella, her women's basketball coach, asked just as Randi was putting down the phone after talking to the fence people.

"Sure, Brad, come on in," she said, completely focused. Women's basketball was a top priority this year. They had to show not only the university and the town's residents that the title they'd won last season wasn't a fluke, but they had the rest of the Division One universities in the country watching them, as well.

They weren't even going to think about the Women's National Basketball Association coaches who were waiting in the wings to make offers to her girls. There'd be time for that later.

If they had another winning season.

"I found a center who can take us all the way home," Brad said, slumping his nearly seven-foot height in a chair near Randi's desk. "Name's Susan Farley."

It was the best news Randi had heard in months.

"Tell me about her."

"She's in Nevada, playing at a junior college. Came from a small high school. Apparently wasn't seen in time to be offered any real scholarship money for her freshman year and couldn't afford to get anywhere on her own."

"She'll have had a lot of playing time."

"You've got that right. She's broken every record the school had."

Randi wouldn't let herself get too excited—but damn, this was as good as a white picket fence for boosting her morale. There was more at stake here than just her track record—or Brad's. She didn't want to let Will down.

"You've spoken to her?"

He nodded. "And to her parents."

"I'll need to see the paperwork, of course, but you have my verbal agreement. Sign her."

"It's not that easy."

Her stomach dropped as Brad frowned at her.

"What's the problem?"

"She was undiscovered last year. She isn't this year."

"She's had other offers."

Brad nodded, and Randi's back straightened. Women's athletics at Montford had been near death when she'd become director. In four short years, she'd taken them to championship status—in basketball and tennis. After six years of schooling and a series of increasingly responsible jobs, she wasn't giving anyone a chance to say that her success was a fluke. Or give them an opportunity to criticize Will for hiring her.

Being the champs in tennis was good, but there was no gate money in it. She needed the basketball success to keep the money flowing. To keep the department alive and competitive.

"How much?"

Brad named a scholarship amount that far exceeded anything Montford had ever offered to a female athlete.

"We have to have her." Randi wouldn't back down. She couldn't.

"If we don't, we'll be playing against her, and I can guarantee we ain't gonna win."

"She's going to be a sophomore?"

Brad nodded.

"How are her grades?"

"Decent, average…mostly C's."

"Mostly? Are there any B's in there, or are we talking D's?"

"Some B's. One or two D's."

Not exactly scholarship quality. Especially by Montford standards.

"She'll have to do better than that if we're going to be able to keep her."

"We have to get her first."

"We'd have her for three seasons."

"So will any other school that gets her."

They stared at each other, Brad's face grim, Randi's determined.

"I'll find the money somehow. You talk her into signing."

Brad's smile was slow in coming, but come it did. "You got it, boss."

Randi felt pretty damn good. Until he left her office and she looked again at her budget and the funds she had available for scholarships. She'd known the figures before she'd spoken with Brad. Been fully aware of them the entire time the coach was sitting in front of her.

The money wasn't there.

But it would be. Somehow.

ZACK WAS IN SURGERY until noon on Friday morning, but the first opportunity he had, he shut his office door, picked up the phone and punched in the number for Randi's office.

He'd behaved like a jerk the night before, leaving without so much as a note. The damage was done, he recognized, but he definitely owed her an apology.

She probably deserved an explanation for his actions—some history might make his position a little easier for her to understand—but Zack didn't share that with anyone. His business with Dawn was over. He intended to keep it that way.

There had to be people who knew, acquaintances with whom they'd associated in Phoenix, but not a soul had ever spoken to him of his wife's indiscretions.

Cassie, of course, knew the truth. However, that didn't concern him because he trusted her and she respected his privacy. She neither asked questions nor answered them.

And no one else in Shelter Valley had reason to be aware of his past. Not unless Randi knew Barbara Sharp, and chances of that weren't great. She'd been off the circuit for ten years.

Besides, he gathered that Barbara and Dawn were keeping things fairly quiet. According to Dawn, after that first meeting at the Phoenix Open, she had never even been to a golf match.

"Randi Parsons." She picked up on the fourth ring.

He pictured her sitting behind her desk, feet raised, as she'd been the other day. Looking sassy and smart and far too delicious for his peace of mind.

"Hello?" she said.

"It's Zack," he finally said before she could hang up.

"Oh."

Not much of a greeting, but probably better than he deserved.

"I, uh, just needed to…" The apology had seemed much easier when he'd run through it in the shower that morning.

Somehow, talking to her, feeling that connection, made the words sound all wrong.

Which was why he felt even more determined to get them said.

"You didn't need to call," she told him. "I'm not an adolescent experiencing her first crush." The even tenor of her voice, the lack of accusation, of tears, took him off guard. "I know what last night was all about, Zack. Don't feel you owe me anything."

"Oh?" *She* might know what that time at her house had been about, but *he* had no idea. He'd never lost control like that in his life.

"We're both consenting adults," she went on. "We both enjoyed ourselves and…and then we were done."

Right. They were done. At least they were clear on that point. He should feel relieved. And he would.

As soon as it really hit him that she didn't expect anything from their encounter—no promises, no permanence.

"Let's not make it messy, okay?" She sounded nothing like the needy woman moaning in his arms the night before.

"Right, okay," he said, sitting up straight at his desk, nodding in complete agreement.

Unless the night had been a disappointment to her. Unless she'd been faking it with him. Unless he hadn't been man enough to satisfy her, either.

"Is there anything else?" she asked.

Zack didn't like being brushed off any more than he liked his irrational and irresolute thoughts. It wasn't like him. He'd never been so uncertain in his life, had considered himself a confident, capable man, one who could handle whatever came his way—until Dawn had dropped her little bombshell on him.

"Uh, yeah, there is something else," he heard himself saying.

"What?" She didn't seem nearly as eager to continue talking to him as she was to get off the phone.

"We did *both* enjoy ourselves last night, didn't we?"

There was total silence on the other end of the line. Zack held his breath, telling himself it didn't matter. He knew he was all man. That he was completely capable of pleasing a woman. He'd pleased several since Dawn had left. And had them calling him for more.

"Didn't we?" he pushed.

"I..."

"Randi?"

"Dammit, I can't lie to you. Yeah, okay? Speaking for myself, I did enjoy it."

Sitting back so hard, his chair rocked, Zack grinned.

"And so did you," she added with as much attitude as she'd shown on the basketball court the other day. "A man has a hard time hiding such things, doesn't he?"

With that last little dig, she hung up on him.

Pleased with the way that had gone, Zack hung up, too. But as he went through his day, giving checkups and shots, spaying a couple of young cats, the conversation played itself over and over in his mind. And what pleased him wasn't that she'd been as insistent as he was on considering last night simply a one-time fling, but that she hadn't been able to lie about the pleasure he'd given her.

It didn't occur to him until he was playing catch with Sammie later that night that giving her pleasure didn't mean a whole lot if he hadn't given her *enough*. If she didn't want more.

Which made him determined to stay away from her. He didn't need the challenge—or the insecurity—of continually wondering whether she was satisfied. Whether she'd tired of him yet.

No, he didn't need Randi Parsons.

He was going to be jogging in the other direction. Fast.

BARBARA SHARP looked across the dining table at Dawn, afraid to believe she'd finally found a relationship that could withstand the rigors of her career. Afraid to believe she'd found someone who wasn't the least bit intimidated by her, someone who didn't give a damn whether she won her next match or not—other than to be happy for her because Barbara wanted to win.

Afraid to believe, after a lifetime of being alone, that she'd found someone who loved her for the person she was inside.

"I'm telling you, you've got to smile more when you're in the public eye," Dawn was saying as she buttered her half of the bagel they were sharing. They'd been talking about the not-always-favorable public perception of Barbara. Dawn knew it bothered her, and as an advertising executive, Dawn also knew how to fix things.

Barbara had already slathered her own half-bagel with cream cheese.

"I'm concentrating when I'm in the public eye," she said, trying to meet Dawn's gaze head-on. But failing. Dawn was right; Barbara had always been uncomfortable about the public demands of her career.

She wanted to play golf. And go home. She didn't

want to give anything more of herself than her performance on the course.

"You've got a beautiful smile, Barb," Dawn said, her voice softening. "It was the first thing I noticed about you."

Barbara did glance up then, wondering how she'd ever gotten so lucky. She'd not only found her soul mate, but had her feelings returned tenfold.

"Are you ever sorry?" she asked, studying the half-eaten bagel on her plate. At first, when everything was so new, Barbara had been confident that Dawn was happy. But now...

"No." Dawn's answer was slow in coming. "At least not about being here. With you."

Barbara's breath caught in her throat. She and Dawn had promised each other complete honesty. "What *are* you sorry about?"

Dawn blinked and Barbara knew she was trying not to cry. "I miss Zack."

In through the nose, out through the mouth. Barbara concentrated on each breath, calming herself as her trainer had taught her to do when, as a teenager, she was prone to panic attacks before a big match.

"Miss being married to him, you mean?" She had to know.

"No," Dawn said immediately. The smile she gave Barbara melted Barbara from the inside out. "I love you, you know that," Dawn said quietly.

"It's not something I take for granted."

"I know. Me, neither."

Their eyes met, reminded each other of promises made—promises meant—and Barbara could breathe again.

"About Zack," she began. She wanted Dawn to be happy, whatever that took.

"I'm not in love with him," Dawn explained, frowning. "But I do love him. He was my best friend for a lot of years."

"I can understand that."

Strange thing was, Barbara could. She'd been best friends with men her entire life—until Dawn. She appreciated the way their minds worked; they knew what mattered and didn't matter. They weren't catty. They didn't gossip the same way women did. She respected their strength.

Other than Dawn, Randi Parsons was the only woman Barbara had ever considered a true friend. But then, her friendship with Randi had always been asexual, just like her friendships with men.

"Have you tried calling him?" Barbara asked as the silence stretched.

Dawn nodded.

"He still doesn't forgive you?"

"I'm sure he doesn't, and I don't blame him. I was unfaithful to him."

"And you've been punishing yourself for it ever since."

Dawn looked up, tears in her eyes. "It was wrong. I've been so unsure about myself my whole life, but the one thing I knew, the one thing I could count on, was my honesty.''

''You weren't being dishonest, hon. You were struggling to find out who you were. Think of how confused you were, how hard you fought to be someone you weren't. And as soon as you knew for sure, you told him.''

Barbara had a hard time forgiving them for those months of discovery, as well. Sometimes she felt so responsible, as though it was her fault Dawn had left her husband, her fault Dawn was there with her, living a life for which she had to take so much heat.

She'd known, the moment she met Dawn, that this was the woman she'd been waiting to meet. She'd known she had to pursue her, see if there was any chance Dawn just didn't know about herself yet. She'd needed to make sure she wasn't reading things all wrong.

But she'd hated herself for doing it, just the same.

She hated to think about those months when Dawn had been her lover—and Zack's, too.

''The sad thing is,'' Dawn murmured, her thoughts turned inward, ''I'm afraid he blames himself.''

''For what?'' Barbara asked. ''The fact that you're with me? What does that have to do with him?''

''He seems to think he did something to drive me here.''

''That's crazy.''

''I know.''

''The man needs to be educated.''

"I know."

Their eyes met again. Filled with understanding. With acceptance of the choices they'd made. Choices that were right for them. Choices that much of the world would not forgive them for.

CHAPTER EIGHT

THE PET-THERAPY CLUB'S first outing was on the second Thursday in February. They took a couple of vans from the school into Phoenix, Zack and Randi both driving. The students were all riding with their companions, human and canine, having paired up two students per dog in the parking lot at Montford. Randi was following Zack who, looking far too good in jeans and a short-sleeved sweatshirt, had the rest of the students and their dogs in his van.

It had been two weeks since she'd slept with him. Two weeks since she'd seen him. After that fateful phone call the next day—the one during which she'd been hell-bent on not hearing an apology from him—they'd only communicated by answering machines.

"You aren't taking a dog, Coach?" Renee asked from the bench seat directly behind Randi.

Randi glanced at her passengers in her rearview mirror. Renee, short, slightly heavy, had paired up with Valerie, a tall skinny quiet girl who hadn't said a word since she'd stuck her name tag to her shirt.

On the seat behind them were Marisa and Beth, both homespun girls who wore no makeup and appeared to be inseparable.

"No," Randi said to Renee, but she wasn't looking at the girl. She was sharing her focus between the road and the large canine on the seat between Valerie and Renee. He—or was it a she—seemed placid enough. But that mouth…and you never knew when… "I, uh, have to supervise," Randi continued in her most authoritative teacher's voice. "You guys are my responsibility and I need to be available if anyone has problems."

Renee nodded.

Beth and Marisa, chatting quietly in the back, apparently had their dog on the floor at their feet. Randi couldn't see him.

Palms sweaty, she concentrated on the license plate in front of her. On the van Zack was driving. The dogs were on leashes. They were *trained* to be nice to people. To heal people.

The license plate was a boring one—123EOE. She soon tired of trying to make something interesting out of EOE and her eyes drifted a bit higher. To the back of the driver's head. Or what she could see of it through the six other heads in that van. Nine, counting the dogs.

Wiping first one palm and then the other on her black leggings, Randi thought about how she and Zack had barely spoken that morning. A brief greeting—minus eye contact—and then they'd been busy with their charges. Hers human, his canine.

Randi was glad. She'd been dreading the meeting. She'd been afraid things would be awkward between them. But no, it had been all business, as though neither of them knew what the other looked like naked.

She'd worn a longer-than-usual thermal shirt today, one that fastened with little hooks and eyelets all the way up the front, just to make herself less accessible.

Yeah, right. Or had she wanted to remind him of the bra he'd removed so skillfully that night…?

Okay, the man turned her on. She'd be a fool to deny it. But she'd made her decision. She loved her life. Was comfortable. Contented. She'd faced enough disappointments, the loss of her golf career being a major one, and managed to survive. Opening herself to a new world of hurt didn't seem smart.

Or maybe she didn't have the courage.

Shaking her head, Randi pulled into the nursing home, parking next to Zack. Randi Parsons wasn't afraid of anything. Growing up with four brothers had seen to that.

"Something wrong, Coach?" Renee asked.

"No." Randi bit down on the lie. "You guys ready?" she asked, meeting everyone's eyes in the rearview mirror.

She climbed out of the van with a chorus of *yeah*s ringing in her ears. And terror in her heart.

Zack. Dogs. And a nursing home. It didn't get any worse than this.

WITH SAMMIE AT HIS SIDE, Zack watched as his charges moved off to their designated hallways, eager to embark on the afternoon's work. The dogs were eager, too, their ears at attention, their tails wagging, as they trotted beside their companions.

Zack didn't worry about them. The dogs knew the drill. The students would be just fine.

He wasn't so sure about their supervisor.

Like him, Randi watched the students and dogs head off—but from a slightly greater distance than Zack. She was barely inside the door of the nursing home.

Sammie tugged on her leash.

"Okay, girl, we'll go," Zack said, looking at Randi. Her eyes skated back and forth, landing nowhere, as though she was trying her best not to see anything. Not the nursing home or its patients. Not the dogs. And certainly not him.

Zack couldn't just leave her like that.

He wanted to believe his motives were completely altruistic as he approached her, but he knew they weren't. He had never obsessed about a woman as much as he'd obsessed about Randi these past two weeks. Not even Dawn.

"Have you ever been to a nursing home before?" he asked softly.

Not quite the greeting he'd have liked, but much better than the nothing they'd managed to that point.

She nodded, stepped back a pace. Swallowed. "My grandfather died in one a couple of years ago."

So that explained her discomfort. "I'm sorry," he told her. "You should have said something."

"It's no big deal. I'm fine."

"You don't look fine."

She shrugged off his concern and he wondered if that was a habit of hers, to make light of the things that bothered her. Sammie pranced around his feet; Randi took another step backward. "I'm just looking for a central location to hang out in case anyone has problems," she said.

"No one's going to have problems," he told her. "These dogs are all veterans to the work, but also to this particular home. The patients here are like family to them."

She smiled, but her expression failed to convey any pleasure. "Still, I need to wait someplace…"

"There's a lounge at the end of this hall," he told her, pointing to his left. "They have vending machines, some couches, a television. We can find you there when we're finished."

"Thanks." She looked almost longingly down the hall. "But I should probably be more accessible than that."

Sammie moved, snorting impatiently, and Randi jumped back an inch or two.

"She's just eager to get to work," Zack explained, frowning. Randi was exhibiting signs of real fear.

Sammie moved again. And so did Randi. And he suddenly had a feeling he was on to something he wasn't supposed to know. He remembered the first meeting of the pet-therapy club. He'd had Sammie and Bear with him.

And she'd hung out in the back of the room.

"You're afraid of them, aren't you?" he said softly.

"Of what? Nursing homes? Of course not," she said quickly. "I mean, they stink—ugh—but there's nothing to be afraid of."

"Not all the wards stink," Zack said. "Only the ones with incontinent patients. And I wasn't talking about nursing homes. I was talking about dogs. You're afraid of dogs."

"No, I'm not," she retorted, her chin lifted as she turned a challenging gaze on him. His eyes held hers, steadfast, telling her he'd seen more of her than most people did.

Her eyes dropped. "Okay, so maybe I am. A little. They have such big mouths."

"All the better to kiss you with," Zack teased, understanding now why she'd been so adamant about canceling the pet-therapy club. It hadn't been because she was impervious to the needs of others, but because she'd known this day was coming. She'd known she was walking into something she couldn't handle.

But she'd walked into it, anyway. Silently. Alone. Forcing herself to face her demons.

As much as he admired her for that, he didn't want her to face them alone.

Zack looked around her and down the hall.

"Damn!" he cried suddenly. "Take this, please."

She took Sammie's leash from him automatically before she'd even realized what he'd handed her. And he was gone before she had a chance to hand it back.

RANDI WAS SO ALARMED at what Zack might have seen, it was a full two minutes before she started to worry about the dog in her care. She stood no closer to Sammie than she'd been when Zack was there. But now she was in charge.

Not that she could count on the dog to know that. Dogs had minds of their own. They did what they wanted when they wanted. They minded their owners when they felt like it—and attacked without warning. They peed when they wanted to, as well.

They were completely unpredictable.

Fortunately, after Zack ran off in such a hurry, Sammie had decided to sit quietly where he'd left her. No more prancing or snorting.

If she hadn't been afraid of drawing attention to herself, Randi would have thanked the dog.

What on earth was keeping Zack?

And where were all those avid students of hers when she needed them?

On their assigned wards, where they belonged, she reminded herself.

"Excuse me," she said as a caregiver passed en route from one ward to another. She'd just come from the direction Zack had headed.

"Yes?"

"The man I'm with left here in kind of a hurry. He went that way." She pointed with her free hand. "Do have any idea if there's anything wrong?"

"Is he a patient here?"

"No. We, uh, brought some dogs in to—"

"Oh, you're looking for Zack."

"Yeah."

"He's in the second room on the right, chatting with Mr. Clearstone. They were debating whether or not the Suns have a chance to make it to the playoffs this season."

"Depends on whether or not Kidd stays healthy," Randi answered automatically, her mind spinning.

What kind of game was Zack playing here?

"It's funny, you know," the caregiver said, apparently not in any hurry to move on. "Mr. Clearstone loves Sammie and was asking Zack where she was. He said she was busy working, but that he'd bring her by soon."

"She's not working yet," Randi said, but she was thinking of some choice words for Dr. Zack Foster.

What kind of doctor did he think he was, anyway? A psychiatrist?

Well, if that was it, then he'd damn well better get to work on himself. A guy who had to sneak out of a woman's house in the middle of the night sure had some hang-ups that needed attention.

Sammie's big brown eyes followed the worker as she headed into the ward across the hall, and if Randi didn't know better, she'd have thought there was longing in the dog's expression.

"You'll need to speak with your owner," she told the dog when Sammie turned those big brown eyes on her. "And if I were you, I'd be good and mad at him."

Sammie sat still.

She noticed a chart, listing the week's meals, posted on the wall. Everything on it was mushy. That must be the dining room straight ahead.

"Don't be getting mad before he's back," Randi added quickly, before the dog could get any ideas. "I had absolutely nothing to do with this and I'm not any happier about the situation than you are."

The dog continued to stare at Randi, as though listening, maybe even waiting for more. And because, when she talked, Sammie seemed content to stay put, Randi said, "So does the smell bother you at all?" And then, "No, probably not. You roll in disgusting stuff. I've seen your kind."

Another caregiver passed by, this one with her arms full of what looked to be men's clothes.

Sammie gazed after her, moving her front paws around a little, as if she planned to follow the older woman into the ward.

"Come to think of it," Randi said, desperate to keep the dog in place even if it meant talking to her, "you probably *like* the smell in here."

An old woman shuffled by, wearing light-blue

polyester pants and a bathrobe with only one big button fastened across her chest. And fluffy blue slippers. She was carrying a baby doll.

"There, there," she murmured to the "child" in her arms. "There's no reason to be afraid. It's just Sammie."

Randi smiled at the woman, hoping her face didn't look as stiff as it felt. That last week of her grandfather's life, when the family had practically lived at the nursing home, Randi had steered clear of the Alzheimer's ward. She'd steered clear of every room but the private one that housed her dying, though completely lucid, grandfather.

After his last stroke he'd been too disabled to be cared for at home, but he'd insisted on leaving the hospital. He'd only been in the home a month before he died.

The old woman passed by again, a little closer this time, her attention almost exclusively on Sammie.

"See?" she said to the doll she held so carefully. "Sammie won't do anything but love you." And then she whispered, "But not as much as I do. You know Mommy loves you best."

Sammie wagged her tail as the woman came closer, and Randi smiled at the woman again, though much more nervously. She wanted the woman to go quietly away before Sammie took it into her head to move.

She looked around for anyone who might be in charge of the dotty old woman and started to sweat.

Sammie wagged her tail so hard it was banging the nondescript tile floor. Randi wondered if it hurt, but if it did, Sammie didn't seem to care.

Maybe dogs didn't have feeling in their tails.

Maybe the woman would go away.

Maybe Zack would hurry up and get back. She looked down the hall in the direction he'd disappeared, renewing her anger with him.

What the hell was he thinking, abandoning her like this? If this project was so special to him, shouldn't he be here doing it, rather than leaving this moment to her, a complete novice—and one who'd just admitted her very personal shortcomings in this area?

She'd given him credit for a whole lot more sense than that.

"Would you like to pet the puppy, dear?"

Randi watched in horror as the old woman leaned down, putting her doll's hard plastic hand on Sammie's head. Randi tightened her grip on the leash, even as she prepared to drop it and pick up the old woman if Sammie became a problem.

She could save the lady. She couldn't handle the dog.

Sammie cocked her head, tail still wagging, and sat patiently while the old woman and her "baby" took turns petting her neck.

"Good Sammie," the woman crooned in a quavery voice. "See, dear, I told you there was nothing to be afraid of."

The woman eventually left—apparently her doll

had dirtied its pants—without ever seeming to notice that Randi was even there.

Sammie was still sitting right where Zack had left her.

Amazing.

"How'd she do, Sam, my girl?" Zack's voice came from behind Randi.

She spun around as the dog barked and flew over to greet Zack.

"What on earth were you thinking—"

"I know, girl," Zack said, bending down to rub the dog behind both ears. "These things take a while."

Sammie barked again.

"She says you did just fine," Zack reported, finally meeting Randi's eyes.

She meant to stay angry with him for a good long time—and to let him know it, as quickly and emphatically as possible. But then she realized she was still holding Sammie's leash. The dog had moved and Randi hadn't jumped out of her skin.

"Here," was all she said, handing Zack the leash. "You keep it."

He started off down the hall, Sammie at his heels. Randi had no choice but to follow him.

"I can't do this! I'm not trained. I'm not even comfortable."

Zack turned, although he didn't stop walking. "You've already done everything you have to do. You stand. Sammie works."

"But what if…I mean, we were lucky she didn't try anything back there, but—"

"Relax," Zack said. "I'll be right beside you the entire time."

"Yeah, so I've noticed," Randi muttered.

"I promise," Zack said.

Their eyes met, and in spite of the jolt that went straight through her, Randi wasn't sure she could believe him, wasn't sure she could trust her own judgment.

"I don't make a promise unless I intend to keep it," he said, as though reading her mind.

They'd reached the doorway of a room, and Sammie, apparently recognizing the person inside, pushed her way in. Figuring that as long as she was a leash's distance away she wouldn't actually have to get near the dog, Randi followed her in.

But not without glancing over her shoulder to make certain Zack was indeed as good as his word.

He was. He was so close behind he almost bumped into her when she stopped in her tracks.

They visited four people over the next forty-five minutes. And Zack had been correct. All Randi had to do was stand there. Sammie did the rest.

If Sammie hadn't been a dog, Randi would have fallen in love with her on the spot. The dog actually seemed to sense what people needed. And then, even more amazingly, gave it to them. Whether it was antics, kisses, or just sitting quietly to let herself be pawed. For each room she entered, for each person she visited, Sammie became a different dog.

"Watch this," Zack said, taking the leash from Randi as Sammie drew them to the door at the end of the ward. "Rick's a quadriplegic. He was in a serious accident, suffered a spinal cord and neck injury and lost the use of almost everything but his eyes...."

Sammie pushed open the partially closed door, but rather than heading boldly into the room as she had with all her other friends, she stopped still, standing in the doorway, watching the occupant of the room intently.

Randi's stomach, every nerve in her body, tightened. She had a bad feeling about this.

"Maybe we should go," she whispered to Zack before she'd even seen what was waiting for them in that room.

Only when Zack shook his head, again whispered, "Watch," and nodded at Sammie, did Randi notice the dog's wagging tail.

She heard the man before she saw him. Or at least she assumed that hissing sound was coming from the room's occupant. As she moved around so that she was on the other side of Zack, able to see the entire room, she had her suspicions confirmed. The man was making those sounds with his mouth.

And the effort seemed to be costing him terribly. His face was beet-red. His knuckles, where they rested on the wheels of his chair, were white.

His chair was beside the window on the far side of the room. There was a bed with a lot of medical contraptions around it between him and them. At the end of the bed was one high-backed orange vinyl chair with scratched wooden arms. A four-drawer dresser completed the decor.

"Sssssss…Sssss."

"What does he need?" Randi asked urgently. "Can't you help him?"

Zack merely shook his head.

Sammie appeared to be waiting for something, too.

"Sssssss."

Randi turned to leave. She couldn't stand to watch this torture.

"Wait." Zack's hand came out, grabbed Randi's arm.

"Sssss…Sssssss."

In all her dealings with Zack, most particularly throughout that whole unforgettable night, she'd found him to be sensitive and aware. Still, she couldn't be a party to this.

"Sssss…Sssss…Ssssssss."

Rick couldn't be more than thirty. With his chiseled features and thick dark hair, he must have been one gorgeous guy before his accident.

Watching him struggle so helplessly tore at Randi in a way she'd never experienced.

"Sssaaammmmeeeeee."

The dog bounded into the room, jumping up, her paws in Rick's lap as she licked his face.

That face turned to Zack, the clear, intelligent green eyes filled with triumph.

"We're going to have you giving lectures again," Zack said, stepping into the room to clasp the other man's shoulder. "You mark my words."

Randi remembered that Zack said he never made a promise he couldn't keep. And suddenly, noting the look of determination—of belief—in Rick's eyes, Randi had no doubt that he would indeed speak all his thoughts again someday.

Rick let his eyes light on Randi, full of question.

Never had she seen a pair of eyes so expressive.

"This is Randi," Zack said, pulling her more fully into the room. "She's a friend of mine."

Randi was too busy smiling at Rick to correct Zack, to remind him that they were merely co-supervisors of a pet-therapy club. Too busy to squelch the brief flash of pleasure she felt at hearing herself described as his friend.

Rick blinked rapidly, startling Randi. Zack, however, watched the man, as though listening to words that Randi couldn't hear.

Looking toward his right hand, Rick smiled.

And then so did Zack. "Sammie," Zack said. "Right."

Immediately, Sammie left Rick's lap to move to the right side of Rick's chair.

And there ensued another lengthy struggle, ending with yet another victory as Rick maneuvered his hand from his wheelchair to the top of Sammie's head. The miracle didn't stop there, though, for with another intense effort, Rick also managed to move his hand down Sammie's spine, petting her.

By the time they'd gathered their students and left the nursing home, Randi had forgotten that she'd meant to give Zack hell....

CHAPTER NINE

"RICK WAS LYING in his bed waiting to die before Sammie came along," Zack told Randi later that evening as they stood together in the back parking lot at Montford. All the students had finally finished talking about everything they'd seen and done and were heading for their dorms. Renee had been the last to leave, and only then after saying goodbye to her canine companion a half-dozen times.

"He refused to cooperate, always closing his eyes whenever anyone came near him."

"His only means of communication," Randi commiserated. She was standing by her driver's door. "It was all the control he had."

Zack nodded, unable to describe how horrible it had been to see the man lying there. It had sure put his own problems in perspective.

"One day, when I was at the nursing home with Sammie, she barked right outside his door. A nurse happened to be in there at the time, filling his feeding tube, and he not only opened his eyes, but kept looking at her and then at the door."

"So you took Sammie in?" Randi asked, her beautiful brown eyes alight with interest.

"I did. That time and a few others. About three months ago the doctors told me there was every neurological reason to hope Rick could regain use of at least some of his motor skills. He may not ever walk again, and any improvement is months of work and struggle, much as you saw today. But it can happen."

"What did he do when they told him that?"

"They'd already told him. But when they told me and I talked with Cassie, we came up with the idea of letting Sammie help him." He leaned a hip against the hood of her Jeep. "The next time I took her to see him, I wouldn't let her in the door until he made an effort to call her. What started out as merely spittle dripping from his mouth became his first word just a couple of weeks ago."

"Sammie was his first word?"

Zack nodded, grinning. Sammie, hearing her name, barked from her seat in his Explorer. Which sent up a roar of agreement from four of her canine companions. Bear was the only dog who remained placid, lying down on the front passenger seat, apparently too exhausted from his day's work to bother with anything.

"You'd better get them all home to their dinners," Randi told Zack, eyeing the Explorer uneasily over her shoulder, as though four thousand pounds of steel wouldn't be enough to keep those hungry dogs away from her if they decided they wanted to get out.

Someday he'd show her that all she needed was a look to keep a trained dog in its place.

"You did well today," Zack said.

"I didn't do anything but stand there."

"I meant with Sammie. You handled her like a pro."

"Yeah, well..." He could see that her eyes were sparking with anger as she gazed up at him. "I have a bone to pick with you about that. No pun intended."

"Go ahead." He could take it. Besides, he was rather enjoying her show of passion. It might not be of the sexual variety, but at the moment it was better than nothing.

"What you did, leaving me alone like that, especially in a place like that, was beyond foolish."

He waited, still leaning against her Jeep. She had more to say; he could see it in her eyes.

And he probably deserved at least some of it. But Sammie had had a job to do and in this particular case, she could only have done it if he left.

"Do you have any idea what could have happened?" Randi asked, her short blond hair adorable as it bounced around her face. "This senile old lady came up to us. She was totally incapable of helping herself if something went wrong. She could have stepped on the dog's toes or pulled her hair, and I'd have been completely helpless to prevent Sammie's retaliation."

"Have you ever tried stepping on Sammie's toes?" Zack asked lazily.

"Of course not." She crossed her arms in front of

her chest. Those little eyelet things keeping her shirt together had been distracting him all day.

"Pity. If you had, you'd know Sammie wouldn't have done anything but sit there."

She thought about that for a moment. "And I suppose you're going to tell me she'd have reacted the same way if her hair had been pulled."

"You're quick."

"So answer me this, Mr. So-sure-of-yourself, what would've happened if she'd decided to follow you into the ward? Or run after a cart of food? Or—"

"She wouldn't have stood up from that spot on the floor even if she had to wet herself."

Randi looked silently from him to the dog. "You somehow told her to sit and stay before you left," she muttered.

Zack nodded, moved his hand down sharply and to the right. "This means sit and stay."

"You knew I was perfectly safe."

"Yes."

"It still wasn't very nice."

"Probably not," he agreed. "But as stubborn as you are, there wasn't any other way I could think of to prove that you don't need to be petrified every time we go on one of these outings."

Randi's eyes met his for a long moment.

"Thank you," she finally said, her expression completely serious.

"You're welcome."

She glanced over her shoulder to the dogs in his

vehicle. "If you don't get them home soon, they may be wetting themselves all over your Explorer."

It was the second time she'd dismissed him. He still wasn't ready to go.

"Have dinner with me."

Randi looked him straight in the eye. "No."

"Why not?"

"I don't think it's a good idea. You know—been there, done that."

He moved a little closer to her, but restrained himself from touching. God, how he wanted to touch her. "I think we should talk."

"We've already done that, too."

"Maybe not enough."

"What's the point?" she challenged him. "The intended goal?"

He took the time to choose his words carefully. He'd told her about not making promises he couldn't keep…

"Things felt a little…awkward today. I'd like to see if we could change that."

"Pretend we haven't seen each other naked, you mean?"

Damn, the woman always managed to catch him off guard. "No."

"Then what?"

"Maybe find a way to be friends."

He took her silence as a good thing.

"We have to work together for at least the rest of this semester."

She nodded, still not speaking as she put one foot on the side runner of her Jeep.

"The thing is, I've been thinking about you far more than I should have these past two weeks." He heard himself telling her a lot more than he'd intended to. "Most mature people discuss certain issues, like what they're looking for or not looking for in a relationship, before they have sex. We skipped that part, and I think it might help us understand each other better if we go back and try to fill in some of the gaps. I know it would make me feel better."

She nodded again, her arms still folded across her chest. "It might help us be friends, instead of lovers, you mean."

He supposed. "Yes, exactly."

"Okay, but let's not go for dinner. I need to get some exercise after the day I just had. You got any Rollerblades?"

"Yeah." Not that he'd been on them a whole lot lately.

"Then how about meeting me at my place in an hour? We'll go for a spin. You can say whatever you have to say then."

Not quite what he'd envisioned, but then nothing with Randi Parsons turned out as he expected.

"Great. One hour." He looked at his watch. "I'll be there."

The exercise sounded good.

RANDI LOVED in-line skating. Flying along the road, her hair tousled by the breeze she created. She loved the freedom. Being on her skates, mile after mile, strengthened her. Not just physically, but mentally and emotionally. Sailing over curbs, through puddles, up hills, down hills, over gravel and debris, she felt as if she could do anything.

Except be immune to Zack Foster. The man skating beside her.

For the first half hour she went as fast as she could, knees bent, shoving off with every muscle she had. She skated hard. But no amount of effort was enough to leave Randi's turmoil about Zack Foster behind. No amount of effort left *him* behind, either.

He was good.

She knew the neighborhoods, knew every hill, every pothole, every street crossing. She'd met every in-line skating challenge Shelter Valley had to offer. He conquered them all on his first go-round. No matter how many sharp turns she took, he was right there the whole way.

She wasn't going to get out of this conversation.

"You've obviously skated a lot," she said, slowing down enough to allow herself to speak. Like her, he was wearing knee and wrist pads, along with athletic shorts and a T-shirt.

Somehow, the outfit that looked prosaic on her was nerve-racking on him.

He came up beside her on the street that ran the entire perimeter of the university. It wasn't quite dusk yet, but the streets were quiet. Only the occasional person out walking a dog or a student cycling by with a backpack. Nothing else to protect her from the conversation to come.

Still, you couldn't get too intimate rolling around on public streets. Even semideserted ones.

"For years, I skated every morning before starting my day."

For years. It was the first time she'd thought of him in terms of life outside Shelter Valley. Adult life. The time between college and now. That was quite a few years unaccounted for.

"By yourself?" she asked. Zack lived alone in Shelter Valley, but that didn't mean he'd always lived alone.

"With my wife."

She stumbled, her skate catching on a rock. She would have fallen if he hadn't been there, grabbing her waist. Steadying her.

The warm touch of his hands on her waist wasn't steadying at all.

"Your wife," she said, instead of a thank-you for his help. She pushed off a little faster, needing the speed again. "I didn't know you'd been married."

"It isn't really common knowledge here," he said, shrugging. "Ben Sanders knows. Cassie knows."

"I'm assuming it's over." It had better be or he was a dead man. Randi didn't sleep with married men. She didn't sleep with men, in the plural, period. And she was never sleeping with him again.

"Of course," he said, gliding beside her, keeping up with her easily.

"How long were you married?"

"Six years."

They were skating side by side down the middle of the street. "Let me guess," she said. "Your move to Shelter Valley coincides with the breakup of your marriage."

"Just about, although the timing was pure coincidence. I'd been dabbling in pet therapy for a couple of years, though with the size of the clinic I was working in in Phoenix, I didn't have a lot of time to spare for it." They slowed gradually as he spoke, taking a pace more conducive to conversation. "When Cassie called," he continued, "offering me half of her practice here—and a chance to be instrumental in helping her get a national pet-therapy program off of the ground—I jumped at the chance."

Randi rounded the corner, crossing one foot in front of the other. "Have any regrets?"

"None."

"Shelter Valley can be a little hard to get used to after life in Phoenix."

He looked at her briefly as they headed down a long straight stretch of road. "I forget, even though you were born here, you spent a lot of time living in the fast lane, too. Was it hard for you to come back?"

The automatic *no* almost passed her lips, but she couldn't seem to say it. Couldn't fool Zack the way she'd been fooling everyone else all these years. Everyone, including herself.

Damn him for making her look at things she'd never seen before. She'd been pretending to be happy, *determined* to be happy, for so long that somewhere along the way she'd begun to believe the fantasy she'd created.

Since Zack's appearance in her life, she'd begun to sense things in her own personality that she hadn't known were there. Dissatisfaction. Longings. A craving for great sex.

"It wasn't coming back that was hard," she finally said after thinking about his question. "I love Shelter Valley, and even after all my travels, all the places I've seen, I know of no other place I'd want to call home.

"There are certain things you can pretty much count on here, you know?" She glanced across at him. "A higher level of morality, for one, which seems to produce higher levels of individual self-worth, high standards. And there's integrity between neighbors, the sense that as a general rule people look out for each other. And not just close friends, either, but the town as a whole."

"'Course, pretty much everyone in this town seems to be close friends."

Randi grinned. "I don't know about that. There may not be all that many of us, but there are still personalities to deal with.

"So what about you? Do you miss Phoenix?"

They turned another corner and Randi slowed down to avoid an oncoming car. Zack, skating behind her, didn't see the car in time to slow down and came up on Randi too fast. He skated into her, his hands on her waist keeping both of them steady and on their feet.

At the touch of those warm masculine fingers spanning her sides, as the jolt of instant awareness shot through her, Randi tensed up again. Damn. For a couple of minutes there she'd actually forgotten she and Zack weren't just friends enjoying each other's company.

"I don't miss Phoenix," Zack said when they were once again back on course. "In the first place, it's close enough if you want to go there or you need something."

"Like a mall?" Randi asked with a chuckle.

"I was thinking more along the lines of a car dealership." He moved behind her as a car passed by. "My Explorer needs to be serviced. It's under warranty, so it has to go to a Ford dealer."

"So that's all you miss about Phoenix? Your Ford dealer?" *Not your wife?*

"Pretty much." He nodded. "Maybe a movie theater now and then. But overall, I much prefer the friendly atmosphere here in Shelter Valley to the anonymity of living in a city the size of Phoenix."

"Me, too."

They left the university behind, turning onto a road that would take them to the outskirts of town. But one that would be fully illuminated with streetlights when dusk finally drifted into night.

"You said it wasn't coming back that was hard, as though something else *was* hard. I'm assuming you weren't referring to the obvious hardship of losing your career."

He'd assumed correctly. Fitting in was hard; being alone was harder. And why hadn't anyone else ever compelled her to think about these things? Why hadn't she forced herself to see them? Why was Zack insisting she study these truths, these questions, when she hadn't even acknowledged that they existed?

She was becoming afraid that there might be more wrong with her life than the lack of a white picket fence.

"I think what was hardest was losing the motivation to reach for the stars," she said now, thinking out loud more than speaking to Zack. "Like maybe I lost the ability to dream."

"Isn't that all just part of growing up?" He skated away from her as he swerved to miss a piece of sagebrush in the road.

"Maybe." She thought about that. "But I'd sure hate to think so." Why live and breathe if it was all going to be a drudgery of sameness?

Yeah. Randi went all out, pushing on ahead, gaining speed as she tried to outdistance that last thought. *Why live, if life was just a drudgery of sameness?* But once the thought was there in front of her, she couldn't escape it. Wasn't that all her life was? A drudgery of sameness. Yet wasn't that exactly what she'd wanted? Sameness? Predictability?

Zack kept pace with her, gliding in silence for several minutes. The air was cool, welcome against her heated skin, evaporating the sweat from her back. She could smell the sweet scent of fabric softener. Someone must be doing laundry in one of the houses set back from the road. Lights shone in most of them.

The streetlights came on.

"You ready to tackle the stuff we came out here for?"

Zack's voice startled her, interrupting her focus on the rhythmic whirr of their skates against the blacktop.

"Not really." It had been his idea in the first place, not hers.

"Would you humor me on this and do it, anyway?"

"I guess."

Turning onto a side street that would take them back toward town, they skated without speaking for a while. What was it he wanted to tell her? And why wasn't he doing it? Had he changed his mind? Decided she wasn't worth it?

Her mind raced with possibilities as her feet sped along the road.

"How do you feel about dating?"

Randi's stomach jumped. Her and him? "You mean in general?"

"Generally, in terms of yourself, but not dating anyone in particular, necessarily."

Had that answer been as convoluted as it had sounded?

"I don't date much," she said, then wished she hadn't. Her dating habits were not any of his business. "Just friends" didn't need to know about dating habits.

"Because you don't want to or because there's no one to date?"

She shrugged, skated around a car parked in the road. "When there was opportunity, I didn't have time, and now that there's time, there's not much opportunity."

"Maybe you—"

"Besides," she interrupted before he could humiliate her by offering advice on finding other men. "I've been living alone for a long time, and believe it or not, I like it that way."

"You never have to wait to use the bathroom," he agreed.

"I can use two of them at once if I want to."

He chuckled. "Let me know when you figure out how to do that."

"I used to think I'd get married someday, have kids." She watched the road, avoiding pitfalls. "But growing up in Shelter Valley, you're kind of brainwashed into thinking that."

"You don't think that way anymore?"

"Nah." Randi shook her head.

"Why not?" he persisted, close beside her. "You're certainly young enough...."

"I just don't see any reason to complicate things." *Don't truthfully see much point in even thinking about marriage and children.* At thirty, her chances were getting slimmer by the day, and they'd been pretty slim before that. "I'm happy. Why mess with that?"

"Happy's good."

"What about you? Have you been out much since your divorce?" *Have you been out at all since then? Or was I a rebound? And obviously not a very good one, since it only lasted one night.*

Which was just fine with her. She'd felt relieved the next morning when they'd come to their mutual agreement. A single enjoyable encounter didn't have to mean any more than that.

"I've been with a few women, nothing serious," he said.

So, she was one of a few. Randi didn't like that any better than being the only one. The first one. The rebound.

She nodded, focusing once again on the rhythm of her skates skimming along the pavement.

"I'm not looking for anything more than short and satisfying," he continued eventually.

What he was or wasn't looking for had nothing to do with her.

"You never want to marry again?"

"No."

Well, that was succinct.

"Maybe you just need some more time to—"

"I don't need any more time," he interrupted her, his voice taking on a harder edge than she was used to. "I've been down that road once. I'm not going back."

"She was that bad to you?"

He was quiet for so long she wasn't sure he'd heard her. Or had she lost him to another time? Another woman?

They came to a corner and had to wait for a car to go by before they could cross the street. He leaned against a lamppost, frowning as he looked at her.

He made a pretty imposing figure standing there, his skates adding another couple of inches to his already impressive height.

"Until the day Dawn asked for a divorce, I thought we had a perfect marriage. A partnership," he said.

The car passed, but Randi didn't move. "What happened?" she asked in spite of herself.

He looked so strong, so indomitable.

"She wasn't as happy as I was. Hadn't been for almost a year. I never even knew." He pushed off, heading across the street that led back to Randi's neighborhood.

"Sounds like you blame yourself for that," she noted, catching up with him.

"I obviously wasn't paying enough attention to

my wife if she was that…unhappy and I didn't have a clue.''

"Or maybe she was just really good at hiding things.''

"She was good at that, all right.''

He was skating so hard she had to really break it wide open to keep up with him.

What things had she hidden? ''Was there someone else, then?'' She couldn't imagine it, knowing him, having slept with him, but that was the most obvious reason for a breakup.

"Yes.'' The word was bitten out so painfully Randi decided to let it go.

He'd not only been blindsided, he'd been betrayed, as well. That was rough.

"I can see why it would be hard to trust again after something like that,'' she offered, instead.

The words weren't merely a platitude. She *could* see. She wasn't sure she'd have the courage to risk another relationship after making herself vulnerable to someone in the most intimate way only to have that person violate her trust.

Hell, she wasn't willing to risk a relationship anyway, and she didn't have half as good a reason.

CHAPTER TEN

ZACK AND RANDI skated twice more that week. Sometimes they raced; he hadn't lost to her yet, but his victories were so marginal he knew it was only a matter of time. They kept each other humble with good-natured ribbing. They talked. And laughed a lot.

Randi had a unique way of looking at the world— a combination of realism and naiveté mixed with a healthy dose of humor—that intrigued him.

But there was no touching. No sex. No dating.

Things were just about perfect.

They *would* be perfect just as soon as he'd had enough erotic dreams about their night together to get her out of his system.

Or took a weekend to visit a woman friend of his in Phoenix.

Whichever came first.

"You've certainly been seeing a lot of Randi Parsons," Cassie said the following Friday, a week and a day after that first pet-therapy visit.

They were in the operating room at the clinic, finishing up after exploratory surgery on an overweight twelve-year-old cocker spaniel who'd turned out to have gallstones. She was Cassie's patient, but Cassie had asked for Zack's help. The dog was high-risk, and Zack had more surgical experience.

"We've skated a couple of times, that's all," Zack said, making the last notes on the dog's chart.

Their assistants would be in to clean up as soon as Cassie and Zack vacated the surgery. Muffy, the cocker spaniel, was in recovery.

Zack and Cassie moved together to the little room where Muffy lay, still unconscious.

Cassie checked Muffy's vitals, nodded with satisfaction. Zack, leaning against the counter, watched. His partner, with her masses of long red curls and creamy complexion, was beautiful. There was no denying that.

He might even have been tempted to pursue an exploration of that beauty for himself if he hadn't been afraid of messing up a perfect working arrangement. And if he'd ever had the feeling that there was "someone home" inside Cassie who might welcome his advances. His partner was a top-notch vet, a warm caring person, but she didn't seem to have any passion in her heart. He'd wondered many times if she'd always been that way or if her ex-husband's betrayal had destroyed whatever passion she'd had.

"Just be careful," she said now, slowly. "In a place like Shelter Valley, being seen with anyone more than once will start all the tongues wagging. Everyone will be watching you. Especially since we're talking about Randi Parsons here."

"Why especially Randi?" he asked curiously. He wasn't afraid of gossips. They could talk all they wanted, weave whatever fantasies they chose, but no fantasy was going to change reality. There was nothing going on between him and Randi.

"Because she's the town darling, of course," Cassie said, as though the answer was obvious.

"Because she was a professional golfer?"

"That had something to do with it, sure. She made it big, and that gets attention in a small town like this."

Zack frowned. "You've made it big, too, Cass. And a lot of the professors at Montford are very well-known in their fields."

Cassie grinned at him over her shoulder. "We've got our share of brains, that's true, but how could we help it with one of the country's leading colleges in our backyard?" She turned back to stroke the over-size dog, guiding her gently into consciousness.

They had trained people working for them who usually did recovery detail, but Muffy was special. She belonged to Cassie's former in-laws. The Montfords were direct descendents of the family who'd originally settled Shelter Valley. The Montfords had left Shelter Valley almost two years ago and had only returned this past Christmas. Until two months before, Muffy had been on an extended vacation in Europe with her owners.

"Anyway, it isn't just the golf thing that makes Randi special, or even the wonders she's managed to bring to the women's sports program at Montford. It's really Randi herself. Everyone loves her.''

Zack could understand that. *Love* was a little strong perhaps, but he could see how someone would have a hard time not liking Randi.

''You should have seen her when we were kids,'' Cassie said, smiling as she continued to stroke the dog. ''She'd trot along after those four big brothers of hers, completely certain that she was their equal. Had them all doing her bidding.''

Muffy sighed and Cassie froze, waiting, Zack knew, to make sure the longer-than-normal breath wasn't the dog's last.

He relaxed his tense muscles when Muffy's chest rose and fell again.

''She might have been a tomboy,'' Cassie continued as though they hadn't just had a scare. ''But the way those guys treated her, there was no doubt she was a princess.''

''So how come the two of you never hung out together?''

Cassie shrugged. ''I wore dresses and played hopscotch with the other girls at recess. Randi played baseball with the boys.''

He could picture it easily.

''Quit grinning,'' Cassie said. ''She whomped them all.''

''Good for her.''

''Be careful, Zack.''

Arms folded, Zack crossed one leg over the other. "I told you, there's nothing going on between us."

She didn't look convinced, but turned back to Muffy. "I would've liked to know Randi better," she said. "It always seemed like she'd be so much fun. But by the time we got into junior high, she was training pretty seriously. And I'd met Sam."

"That young?"

"Younger, really, but by junior high we were inseparable."

He'd had no idea they'd been together that long.

"Didn't you ever date anyone else?"

She shook her head, eyelids lowered as she focused on the dog. Zack wondered for a second if she was hiding tears.

"We tried," she said softly. "When we were in high school, the youth minister at the church asked us to spend some time with other kids. He said that either we'd find out we *weren't* meant to be together, or we'd be more committed than ever. Said it could only strengthen our relationship if we found out there truly wasn't something—or someone—else for us."

"So you went out with different kids?"

"Yeah, but we still couldn't think about anyone but each other. And yes, it did strengthen our relationship."

She slipped a finger under her eye. Damn. He'd been right about the tears.

"Or at least I thought it did," she finished.

What remained of Zack's faith in marriage took a

nosedive. If two people who'd been together as long as Cassie and Sam before tying the knot, whose lives and hearts were that intertwined, couldn't make a go of it, there were no guarantees anywhere.

No way to ensure you didn't make the same mistake twice. Live through the same agony twice.

Except never to try it again.

"You ever think about remarrying?" he asked, his voice low.

Cassie shook her head, still gazing down at Muffy. "Doesn't seem to be much point."

Muffy's eyes, opening slowly, looked glazed. Which was to be expected. Except that Muffy's were rolling up into her head. Zack joined Cassie at the table, listening to the dog's heart.

"It's a bit fainter than I'd like, but steady," he told her.

They worked together for a few more minutes, adjusting Muffy's IV, making the dog as comfortable as possible.

"Sam and I bought her," Cassie said, giving up on hiding her tears as one dripped off the end of her nose onto the rounded side of the dog's belly.

"She was yours?"

"No." Cassie petted the dog softly, long strokes from the top of her head to her hip and back again. "Sam's mom just seemed so sad after he left home. He was their only child—a big part of their lives. We figured Muffy would help fill the gap."

"Pet therapy even back then, huh?"

Cassie's grin was watery, but it was there. "Yeah, I guess," she said. "Not that I had any idea what I was doing."

"Or maybe you did," Zack said. "You just didn't know it yet."

Muffy continued to hold on, and another hour slipped by. The dog's eyes were staying open—even focusing a little.

"We might win this one, Cass," Zack said after checking the spaniel's vitals one more time.

A few more tears escaped as she stood with the dog's head in her hands. "Thank you."

"Hey," he said, knocking her lightly on the shoulder. "You did most of the work."

"Standing around supervising isn't work."

"No, but it was the love that saved her. Pet therapy works both ways, you know."

She nodded, still tending to the dog, but he could see her slowly relaxing. So much of who Cassie was she kept hidden inside. Zack ached for her.

It was a damn good thing Sam Montford hadn't bothered to show his face in his hometown last summer for the dedication of his great-grandfather's— and namesake's—statue. Zack would've had to kill the man for what he'd done to Cassie.

Surely robbing a woman of her soul was punishable by death.

"I know you're not taking me seriously about Randi," Cassie said a few minutes later when it was obvious that Muffy had made it through the danger zone and Zack was preparing to leave. "But *please* be careful, Zack. You don't know this town like I do. You hurt her and they'll never forgive you."

"I'm not going to hurt her."

He wasn't going to do anything to her.

Except beat her the next time they raced.

SHE'D GONE to her alumni. They'd given her all the money they had available until their next fund-raising event, a black-tie affair that was scheduled for September—far too late for Randi to sign Susan Farley.

Her community-allotted funds had already been spoken for. The track team got new uniforms. The volleyball and softball coaches needed new equipment.

And she'd just gone to the dean of students for a raise for her coaches. They were still making less money than Montford's men's coaches and they shouldn't be.

Where in hell was she going to find the money to offer Susan Farley the kind of scholarship that could compete with what the girl would get elsewhere?

Randi had a Montford education to offer. Which, in itself, carried a lot of weight. But only to someone who needed it. If Susan was as good as Brad said— and Randi knew she was just because Brad said so— then the girl was probably looking to turn pro. A school that could offer her hope in that direction would ultimately mean more to Susan than a highly acclaimed academic degree.

"Excuse me, Coach Parsons?"

Randi was on the floor of her office, stretching. Thinking. "Yes?" she said to the softball player hovering in her office doorway.

"I'm Jan Walters. Coach Randall said you wanted to see me."

Coach Lauren Randall was Montford's head softball coach.

"Yes." Randi stood up. "Come in, Jan."

Damn. She'd been hoping for another day or two before she had to tackle this one. More accurately, she'd been hoping the problem would disappear before it even got to her.

"Have a seat," Randi told the husky girl shifting nervously from foot to foot just inside the office.

Waiting until the girl chose a chair in front of her desk, Randi closed the office door. Jan watched as Randi took her own seat.

Randi did a lot of tough things in the course of her job. Welcomed most of the challenges, thrived on many of them. This was one challenge she could do without.

"I don't know what this is about, Coach Parsons, but if it has to do with my scholarship, I'll do whatever it takes. I can't lose that money. I'd have to leave Montford for sure."

"You're a junior, right?" Randi asked, buying time. Hoping for some kind of divine revelation to enter her body and come out her mouth.

"Right."

"You've been on scholarship all three years?"

"Yes, ma'am," the young woman said, blond ponytail bobbing as she nodded her head with extra emphasis. She was also chewing her lips.

"How are your grades?"

"Better than they ever were in high school."

"C's and above?"

"B's and above."

Jan was obviously uncomfortable, but she was meeting Randi's gaze head-on. Randi liked that.

Which made the upcoming interview even more difficult.

"You have no idea why Coach Randall sent you to me?" Randi asked.

Jan shook her head. "No, ma'am."

Damn Lauren and her chicken-shit delegating to higher authorities.

And why did I ever think it would be cool to be a higher authority?

"There've been some complaints filed against you, Jan. Enough of them to warrant this meeting."

"Complaints?" The young woman sat forward, her muscular arms resting on the arms of the chair. "From who?"

"Your teammates."

Jan's eyes grew wide. "I've never missed a practice," she said. "The season's only beginning, but I've scored a couple of runs already. Made some good plays. I'm not letting the team down."

"The complaints have nothing to do with your performance on the field."

"Oh." Jan bowed her head.

Well, Randi thought, taking a deep breath. At least they were finally talking about the same thing.

"Have you read your student handbook, Jan?" Randi asked gently.

"Not lately."

"You do realize that sexual harassment can be cause for expulsion from the university, don't you?"

"I haven't harassed anyone!"

"Not really, no," Randi allowed.

"When they say they aren't interested, I leave them be."

"I know, and that's why I'm talking to you, rather than kicking you off the team."

More than anything, Randi hated this. Hated dealing with something she didn't really understand.

She knew the facts. She'd been around people like Jan her entire life. She made her decisions about them on an individual basis; she didn't like or dislike people because of their sexual preferences. She liked them because of *who* they were, not what they were. She didn't particularly understand Barbara Sharp's interest in women, for example, but she didn't judge her, either. She just hated having to poke her nose into other people's intimate lives.

"The thing is, Jan, you've approached so many of your teammates they're all feeling skittish. They don't want to be around you, don't want to have you in the locker room with them."

Head still bowed, Jan didn't say a word.

"Everyone you haven't approached is afraid she'll be next."

"I'm not the only gay woman on the team," Jan said, finally looking up, defensiveness written all over her face.

"Probably not. But you're the only one looking to your teammates for a relationship."

She threw up her hands. "So where'm I supposed to look?"

Oh, God. How did *she* know?

"Aren't there clubs out there? Places you can go to meet other women?"

Jan's gaze pinned Randi. "Would you go to a bar to meet a man?"

"No." And then, "How about the Internet?"

Jan just shrugged.

"I'm sorry I'm not equipped to help you with this one, Jan," Randi finally said. She was still sitting primly at her desk, hands folded on top of it. But she was slowly flexing and pointing her feet under her desk. Wishing she could be straightening the laces on her pristine white running shoes. "But I do know that if you don't stop hitting on your teammates, I'll have to suspend you from the team. This is the only warning you're going to get."

Jan nodded, stood up. "I understand," she said, her mouth turned down with dejection. "Thanks for not canning me right off the bat."

"You're welcome."

Randi stood, too, reaching out to shake Jan's hand.

"You just go out there and do what you're here to do. Make me proud and win me some games."

"Yes, ma'am," Jan said, smiling as she took Randi's hand. "Hey, you wouldn't be interested in an after-game drink, would you?" she asked. "To celebrate that win?"

"Jan—"

"Just kidding, Coach," Jan said, grinning openly. "You're way too old for me."

"Beat it," Randi said, shooing the girl out of her office with a grin.

But the grin faded as soon as Jan had left. Even as a joke, it wasn't the first time she'd been hit on. But she hated it as much now as she had the first time it had happened. Hated that just because she was a talented athlete and wore her hair short, people assumed she might be a lesbian. That they could stereotype her that way, could assume things about her.

She knew reactions like those had been part of the reason she'd been asked out so rarely by men. Some didn't think she'd be interested. Or weren't interested in her because of assumptions they'd made. Some were just plain intimidated by her.

And then there was Zack....

She wanted to go home and call her mom. Or one of her brothers.

She wanted to feel like the princess they'd always taught her she could be.

CHAPTER ELEVEN

THE WHOLE IDEA came about while they were skating. It was a Wednesday evening. The streets were deserted, and Randi and Zack had been talking about movies they'd seen.

There was a new Tom Cruise movie out in the theaters. Randi thought it was going to be great. Zack was pretty sure it wasn't.

"Let's just go see it and settle this once and for all," Zack finally said. They were approaching Randi's house—always their starting point—and because he was going so fast, he swerved in front of her to go up the curve onto her driveway. "You left your lights on again."

She followed right behind, pulling her front-door key out of her pocket. "I always leave my lights on. I told you that. And I'll go only if you promise to buy me a burger if I'm right."

"Let me get this straight," he said, following her into her foyer where he'd left his shoes. "If I like the movie, I have to buy you dinner."

"Just burgers. Take-out. Greasy and bad and nowhere to be had in Shelter Valley."

"Greasy and bad, huh? You're living dangerously, Coach Parsons."

"A girl's gotta do what a girl's gotta do," Randi said, bending down to unfasten her skates.

He'd already removed his. "You're on."

The movie was good. The burgers were even better. Spending the entire evening with Zack was best of all.

Randi decided having a friend was just about the most perfect thing in the world.

Who needed sex?

THE NEXT AFTERNOON the Montford Pet Therapy Club made its second visit into Phoenix. As before, Randi was partnered with Zack and Sammie. They went to a different nursing home, but here, too, Randi saw the changes that came over people when Sammie walked in the door.

The kids, too, were thriving on the experience. When they returned, they asked Zack and Randi if they could possibly schedule a couple more visits during the semester. Zack said he'd see what he could do.

"How often do you visit Rick?" Randi asked after all the kids had left, and she and Zack got ready for their evening skate.

She'd been looking forward to seeing Rick again. And was anxious to find out if he'd reached any new milestones.

"I like to get in at least once a week, but don't

always make it, depending on how busy we are at the clinic. And whether or not Cassie's in town. But I never let it go more than two weeks."

"So you've seen him since we were last there?"

He nodded. "I went last Sunday."

"I would have liked to go." She'd been having dinner with her family, instead. They'd stopped pressuring her about living alone since she'd bought her house, but all of a sudden the little comments had started up again.

He sent her a sideways glance. "You mean that? You'd like to visit him?"

"Yeah. I liked him." Enough to put up with Sammie.

"Then let's do it," Zack said. "I have a feeling he'd really like to see you again, too."

"Okay. When do you plan to go?"

"Tomorrow, if you'd like."

Tomorrow was Friday, and it wasn't as though she had any plans for the weekend. "Okay."

She waved at a woman who was out walking, one of her sister-in-law Becca's sisters. Which meant Becca would be hearing that she and Zack had gone out skating together again. But Randi had been dealing with her family her entire life. She could handle their nosiness and misguided concern. "So how was he?" she asked, returning to their discussion of Rick.

"He's good." Zack coasted around a corner. "He's added another word to his vocabulary—*no.*"

"Good for him!" Randi said. "At least now he can stick up for himself."

"He asked about you."

"Since he only has two words in his vocabulary, neither of which is Randi, how did he ask for me?"

"Same way we have many of our conversations. He kept looking at the door, his eyes asking the questions. I guessed until I got it right."

She wondered how many guesses it took. And where the conversation had gone from there. Zack didn't offer that information and Randi was afraid to ask. Wasn't sure she wanted to know what he'd said about her. If he'd said anything at all. She'd grown up with four brothers. She knew how guys talked.

"Did you tell him I'm going to beat you next time we race?"

"I didn't know that you were."

"Mm-hmm," Randi murmured, grinning.

They'd just arrived at the elementary-and-junior-high-school complex, and Randi skated up on the sidewalk that surrounded the entire school property. Because it encompassed a good-size playground, a track, football and soccer fields and a baseball diamond, the sidewalk was almost a mile long.

"Let's go," she said. "Once around." She was off before he'd agreed, but he was quick. He'd be right behind her.

And that was the idea. Randi wasn't sure she could beat him without a head start. It was an intriguing phenomenon—and an unusual one.

Knees bent, body forward, she pushed off with all her might, wishing she'd thought to spray the bearings in her wheels. Surely she should be getting more reward for her effort.

He was right on her tail and Randi pumped harder. She could beat him. She could do anything she set her mind to. She could beat him. She could do anything…

The mantra continued in her head as she flew around the school, swerving and turning as the sidewalk wound this way and that, taking dips and hills, avoiding stray stones. She approached the last few yards of the impromptu course, and just as she reached the last two squares of sidewalk, Zack whizzed by her.

"Damn." She coasted to a stop, then bent over to catch her breath.

It was something of a salve to her pride to see that he was as winded as she was. That gave her hope.

"I'm rotating and cleaning my wheels this weekend," she panted. "I'll get you next time."

"My wheels probably need maintenance, too," Zack said, starting slowly down the street. Randi went after him and soon caught up with him, wondering if her skates were really the explanation for her loss.

RICK WAS IN HIS CHAIR, out in the hallway, head lolling on his chest, when Randi and Zack arrived the next afternoon. Sammie saw him first, tail wagging as she approached him. She sniffed the limp hand lying on the arm of the chair, licked it. Randi cringed, hoping the dog didn't upset him.

After all, it wasn't as though Rick could pull his hand away.

"Is he sleeping?" Randi asked softly.

"Maybe." Zack shrugged. "But probably not. He can't hold his head up, and without the restraint, it does that."

"Hey, Rick, my man, how you doing?" Zack asked, lifting Rick's head and settling it in the brace attached to the back of his chair as easily as if he was shaking the other man's hand.

Rick blinked once.

"Look who I brought to visit you," Zack said, turning Rick's chair so he could see Randi.

She smiled. Rick blinked three times.

"What's he saying?"

Sammie barked once.

Zack laughed. "I think they're both saying hello." He wheeled Rick's chair into his room. Sammie trotted after them, but stopped just inside the door.

"Sssss…"

"Ssssss…"

Rick tried six times before he managed to say the name. Randi had to bite her tongue not to blurt it out for him.

"Ssssaaaammm." When he finally said it, Randi turned expectantly to Zack's dog. She was smiling as she waited for Rick to receive his hard-won reward.

Sammie continued to sit by the door. Randi looked at Zack, who was standing just to the side of Rick's chair. He shook his head.

Frowning, Randi glanced back at Rick. Because he couldn't smile or frown distinctly, it was hard to tell just what the man was thinking, but it didn't matter. Randi couldn't just stand there.

"Make her go to him," she told Zack. When he didn't move, she moved towards Sammie herself.

"Stop," Zack said.

Rick's eyes were blinking furiously.

"He wants to show you the progress he's made," Zack interpreted.

Confused, Randi stood and watched as Rick's right hand fumbled along the arm of his chair, falling off, then getting back on. It looked as if he was moving his hand forward, toward the little joystick near the end of the arm.

Randi looked at Zack, biting her lip when she saw the intense concentration on his face as he watched the other man. This was as hard for Zack as it was for her, the frustration of not being able to help, of not being able to do for him what he couldn't do for himself.

Except that Rick *could*.

After fifteen minutes of trying, with sweat dripping down the sides of his face, Rick finally got his hand on the joystick. Slowly, with jerking starts and stops, his chair began to move.

A couple of minutes later, Rick was sitting beside Sammie—beside Randi—and as his hand lifted to the dog, as Sammie licked the hand that was petting her so awkwardly, Randi could have sworn she saw a smile on Rick's crooked lips.

RANDI COULDN'T GET the episode out of her mind as they drove back to Shelter Valley that evening. Her opinion of Zack rose every time she was with him. Never had she known a man so strong, so sure and at the same time so compassionate.

Her opinion of Sammie had risen, too. Not that she wanted to be friends with the dog. She didn't. Couldn't believe she'd actually reached for Sammie's collar like that. But she was impressed with the dog's patience. Her ability to help a man who'd had no life left.

As Zack turned his car toward Randi's street, they passed a young boy sitting on his bike at the end of his driveway. He was thin, with short brown hair and very expressive eyes. Randi didn't know him, didn't know who he belonged to and wondered if someone new had moved to town.

"Did you ever see the movie *The Sixth Sense?*" Zack asked.

"No. I wanted to, but I didn't get to Phoenix while it was still playing."

"That boy back there looks just like the kid in the movie. Almost makes me shiver."

"I take it you saw it."

"Several times. It was extremely well-done."

"I'll have to rent it sometime soon."

"You don't need to rent it. I own a copy. You could come by my place later and we can watch it together."

Randi hesitated. "How about if I just borrow it from you sometime?"

"You got other plans tonight?" He looked over at her. Frowned.

"No." But she couldn't go to his house. Too much risk that she might forget her plans. Her decisions. His adamant refusal to consider another long-term relationship.

"It's a movie you shouldn't see alone. At least not the first time."

"I'm always fine alone."

"So, maybe I don't feel like playing catch with Sammie tonight. Come on, take pity on me."

She hated to disappoint him.

And he didn't seem the least bit concerned about their spending an evening alone in his home. This from a man who'd made it very clear that one night with her had been enough.

What was she worried about?

"Can we pick up frozen pizza?"

"Do you ever think of anything but your stomach?"

"I burn a lot of calories."

He looked over at her. She could feel him looking. Could almost feel the touch of his eyes as they roamed her body.

"I'll get a pizza," was all he said.

She'd probably just imagined the rest. She needed to get a grip. Decide on a goal for the weekend. A project. One she could master by Monday. She'd always been good at focusing on her goals.

ZACK HAD THE PIZZA in the oven by the time Randi arrived at his place. She'd not only showered but put on real clothes. A pair of jeans, a blouse. She was wearing shoes that weren't white—they weren't even running shoes. He was barefoot, in a pair of sweat shorts and a T-shirt. Dressed like any of her brothers getting ready for a slovenly afternoon of football.

He looked a hell of a lot better than her brothers ever had in that kind of outfit, but the message came through loud and clear: this evening was nothing special to him. Feeling a little foolish, she took due note.

Sammie greeted her at the door, nudging her hand. Randi smiled down at the dog, patted her head once and moved quickly to the side.

"Stay," Zack told the dog as they moved into the house. Sammie lay down on the tile by the front door, head between her paws.

"Where's Bear?" Randi asked. She was trying to be polite, to show interest in the other members of his household, but mostly she just wanted to make sure she didn't run into Bear unawares. Bear was old. And old dogs were even more unpredictable than the rest of them.

She could still feel the blood trickling down her neck from the edge of her hairline…. A neighbor's old dog had chased her down the sidewalk. The dog had run faster than two-year-old Randi. And jumped at her from behind….

"He's in the kitchen," Zack said, "finishing up his dinner. It takes him a while. Which is why Sammie's out here."

And Randi had thought Sammie's orders were because of her.

"She's not allowed to watch him eat?" she asked, glancing over her shoulder at the dog as she followed Zack around the corner and into the living room.

"She doesn't merely watch," Zack said. "She tries to help him, and he gets a little cantankerous about that."

"Just like a guy," Randi murmured. She wouldn't be going into his kitchen anytime soon.

The house was nice. Only a couple of miles from her own, in a slightly upscale neighborhood. Larger than hers, with lots of windows and a no-stucco finish. It even had a white picket fence. But what it gained in location, it lost in interior decor.

"How long have you lived here?" Randi asked as she looked around. The living room was large—open and airy with big windows—the furniture all leather and new-looking. But…

"Almost a year."

"You have nothing on your walls."

And nothing in his spare bedroom, either.

"I've never been too interested in decorating," he said.

"Well, sure, I can understand that." Sort of. "But don't you have *anything* you've collected through the years? A few photographs, maybe? A trophy?" She peeked into his office, empty except for the desk. "A diploma?"

"I left everything with my ex-wife."

"Everything?" Randi asked, still staring around his virtually empty office. "She finds herself another man and you give her everything *you* own?"

With only a shrug, he led her back down the hall to the spacious living room without giving her a glimpse behind the closed door, which had to be the master bedroom.

She vacillated between relief and disappointment. She'd wondered so many times, as she'd lain in her bed alone at night, where he slept. Tried to picture him there.

He'd provided no visual information to make that any easier.

SHE FINDS HERSELF *another man*... Randi's words haunted Zack as he brought pizza and drinks to the living room, setting everything on the coffee table in front of the couch. Sammie came over to investigate, but at Zack's command, crawled under the coffee table and lay down.

He had to grin as, dog somewhat contained, Randi dug right in, helping herself to a beer and a couple of pieces of pepperoni pizza.

"Mmm. Heaven," she said, taking a healthy bite.

But his grin faded too soon. By his silence, he was allowing Randi to think something that wasn't true. That his ex-wife had left him for another man.

Zack knew he'd had nothing to do with Dawn's choice. That he'd had nothing to do with Dawn's attraction to women. Yet, no matter how many times he told himself that, no matter how clearly he grasped it intellectually, he still *felt* responsible somehow.

Had he not been warm enough for her? Had he lacked understanding? Shown too little emotion?

"Come on, have some before I eat it all," Randi said, motioning toward the pizza with the paper plate in her hand.

Zack sat. He took a slice of his favorite spoil-himself snack—not that he'd tell Randi that or he'd never live it down, not with the ribbing he'd given her earlier—but he was still uncomfortable.

He had a right to his privacy. Owed Randi nothing.

And yet…

"When Dawn told me she wanted a divorce," he began abruptly, "she just dropped it out of nowhere one morning while we were getting ready for work. There was no discussion. Absolutely no hope of

working on anything. She was in love with...
someone else and was filing for divorce that very
day.''

*Great, Foster. Entice the lady with charming din-
ner conversation.*

Not that he was out to charm Randi. Maybe just
ease his conscience a bit.

''What a bitch,'' Randi said between bites. Her
eyes were filled with compassion. God, she was
beautiful.

He bowed his head, picking up a piece of pizza,
holding it.

''She wasn't, really,'' he said, admitting something it had taken him a year to accept. ''Dawn
was—is—a very caring, intelligent woman. She
couldn't help that she met her soul mate five years
after she'd married me.''

''Why was she even looking five years after she
married you?''

Good question.

''She didn't go with a joyful heart,'' Zack said,
instead. ''I could see how much it hurt her to break
up our partnership. How much she wished it could
have been different. I honestly believe she would've
done anything to change how she felt. But...she
couldn't.''

''You're very generous.''

The smirk on Zack's face held no humor. No sarcasm, either. ''I just know my limits.''

''And those are?''

Bear wandered in, sniffed at their feet, at the coffee table, and wandered over to the tile in front of the fireplace to lie down.

"If it had to be over, it was over. She'd laid everything out, sparing herself nothing. And when someone's being humble like that, admitting her wrongs and her needs with such honesty, it's a little hard to have any hope for what just died. I knew I had to accept what she was telling me and move on.

"There was no way I was going through weeks of packing, dividing up what was mine, what was hers. Reliving memories that no longer meant anything."

Randi froze, a flopping piece of pizza on the way to her mouth. "You just walked away."

Zack nodded, took his first bite of pizza.

"You and Dawn never spoke about terms, about anything?"

"Nope."

"Not even through attorneys?"

He shook his head again. "I walked out and never looked back. Several months ago, divorce papers arrived, I signed them, mailed them back, and that was that." And he'd do it exactly the same way if he had it to do over again.

Things didn't matter. They could be replaced.

"She was so selfish that she not only betrayed your relationship but served you with papers giving her everything?"

"No." He continued to eat. He hadn't told her the whole truth, but he still felt better. "I'm entitled to

half of everything. The profit from the sale of the
house, the belongings, a few other assets.''

"So where are they?''

In boxes, in an air-conditioned storage unit, according to the note he'd received through Dawn's
attorney with the final divorce decree. And in a safe-
deposit box in a Phoenix bank.

But because he wasn't prepared to explain to
Randi *why* he was leaving all that stuff right where
it was, because he couldn't tell her why it was only
salt in a wound that was still too raw, he just
shrugged. Again.

"I transferred my half of all the monies into a
separate account the morning I left,'' he said. "I
don't need anything else. Now, how about this
movie?''

Randi gave him an odd searching glance, then sat
back, another piece of pizza on her plate. "I'm
ready,'' she said.

Grabbing the remote control, he clicked on the
large-screen television set and the DVD player, and
sat back to be terrorized with someone else's visions
for a change.

THE MOVIE WAS better than he remembered, the pizza
apparently not as good as it had seemed. Randi's
voracious appetite vanished almost before the opening credits had rolled by.

The first time Zack had seen *The Sixth Sense* had
been with Dawn. She'd been truly frightened, dis-

turbed beyond the vicarious thrill the experience was meant to impart. Somehow she'd had a hard time recognizing that although the story was told extremely well, it was still only a story. Fiction. Entertainment. She'd sunk lower and lower in her seat, eventually falling asleep on his shoulder until the movie was over and they could leave.

If he'd had any idea it was affecting her that strongly, he'd have left long before that. There was no way he would've subjected her to such discomfort, but just like everything else in their marriage, he hadn't had a clue until it was too late to do anything about it.

Dawn hadn't let on. Or he'd never tuned in.

He still wasn't sure which was more accurate.

Maybe they were equally true.

Sammie crawled out from under the table and sniffed around them, looking for crumbs. Finding none, she sat next to Randi, laying her head on Randi's knee.

Randi barely seemed to notice, even patting the dog's head before abruptly pulling both hands into her lap. Eventually Sammie moved over to Zack, and Zack spent the next few minutes attempting to lower his blood pressure a bit.

The movie was hair-raising, he reminded himself. The state of his blood pressure had nothing to do with the woman sitting next to him. Absolutely nothing.

CHAPTER TWELVE

BY THE LAST FIFTEEN MINUTES of the movie, after two hours of sitting next to Randi, feeling her energy, watching her gorgeous body strain with the effort it took to live through a young boy's anguish, Zack was restless. Feeling caged.

No longer sure what was so great about just being friends.

He had dogs. They were man's best friend. What he needed was a woman.

This woman.

And the thing was, judging from the covert glances Randi had been sending him on and off over the past two weeks, she wanted him, too. She'd even dressed up for him tonight. He might not be able to tell when a woman *didn't* want him, but he sure as hell knew when she did.

They'd been great together in bed. Two bodies that fit together perfectly.

He shifted in his seat. The credits were coming up soon. Randi was holding her breath as the movie crescendoed.

Randi snatched his hand as the final scene played

itself out, her fingers practically cutting off his circulation.

Her skin was soft. Vital. He grabbed hold.

God, he wanted her.

And it felt so damn good. To *let* himself just want a woman.

Dawn had done a lot of damage. She'd stripped him to the core. Talking about her tonight had brought it all back. The shock. The inner fears. The unanswered questions. He'd never doubted his ability to have great sex. He had a lusty appetite. What he doubted was his ability to make sure the woman he was with enjoyed herself as much as he did.

Randi had a way of making him feel he could do no wrong.

Sammie, lying under the table again, lifted her head, looked at them, then laid it back down.

As the credits finally rolled across the screen, Zack didn't let go of Randi's hand. She'd finally taken her eyes from the television set—to stare at him.

"I thought we weren't going to do that again," she whispered.

"We aren't going to tie ourselves down with false expectations." They'd been honest, each knowing where the other stood.

She bit her lower lip. Nodded.

Zack pulled her across the cushion separating them. She moved toward him slowly, her gaze fixed on his.

For that moment there was no doubt. No past. No

future. And no more thought. There was only this moment. This woman.

Zack lowered his head.

RANDI WOULD HAVE made love with Zack right there on his couch, she was so far gone. Desire had been building from the moment he'd left her house that night all those weeks ago.

"Not here, not like this," Zack murmured against her throat, giving her delicious chills all the way through her body. He picked her up easily and carried her down the hall to the door that had been closed to her earlier.

Wrapped in his arms, dwarfed by his large body, she felt feminine—and desired. She felt fragile and safe, protected and oh, so precious.

"I didn't get to watch you undress the last time," she said when he placed her on his bed and bent to follow her down.

"And that disappointed you?"

"Not at the time," she admitted with a grin, looking at him with lazy eyes. She felt drugged, sluggish, and yet spurred on by a passion that was raging out of control. "It was only later." She ran her tongue across her lips. "When I didn't have enough pictures in my mind…"

She was lying flat on her back, propped up by a couple of pillows, fully dressed except for the shoes she'd abandoned in the living room. Her nipples were hard, straining against her bra.

He pulled his T-shirt over his head. "You've been trying to picture me naked?"

"Uh-huh." And her memory, even mixed with a heavy dose of imagination, had not done him justice. His chest was magnificent. So firm and muscular that every sinew was outlined.

Dark hair swirled in the middle of his chest, reaching out to encircle both nipples. A trail of it ran down over his abdomen, as well, and beneath, hidden by the sweat shorts he was wearing.

"Keep going," she urged as he stood there, feet apart, hands in the waistband of his shorts, watching her.

"When have you pictured me naked?" he asked, instead.

When haven't I? "Once while we were skating and you were in front of me. Your, um, backside was right there and—"

"Only once while we were skating?" he asked. His eyes glinted with humor. With challenge. And with something much hotter...

"Okay, more than once."

He eased his waistband down an inch. "When else?"

Randi licked her lips for real. He was going to make her pay for her pleasure. That thought made her want it all the more.

"In my office, when I was supposed to be approving the assistant director's budget."

His waistband lowered another inch.

"Once at the grocery store."

Swirls of dark hair were her reward for that one. And a bulge that she was very impatient to see.

To feel.

"When we were at the movie the other night."

He lowered his pants another inch.

"When I was lying alone in my bed at night."

His shorts dropped to the floor. "Lady," he said, sliding down beside her, taking her in his arms. "You aren't alone in bed tonight."

"Thank goodness," she whispered as he took her mouth in a kiss so consuming she was no longer sure where she was.

Except in his arms.

And that was enough.

Zack loved her slowly, undressing her, touching her gently, everywhere. Exposing nerve endings she didn't know existed. The undersides of her elbows had never before been connected to the pit in her lower belly. Nor had the backs of her knees. But when Zack touched them, kissed them, ran his tongue along them, her belly tightened with excruciating need.

"You are so beautiful," he said as though he was worshiping her. "So firm." He caressed her arms, the tops of her thighs. "And so womanly." His fingers delved slowly, intimately, inside her.

"Make love to me," Randi whispered desperately. He was driving her crazy. Making her hurt with need in places that weren't supposed to hurt. Places that didn't normally feel pain.

"I am, Miranda Parsons, I am."

And he did.

He took her traditionally the first time, climbing on top of her, holding his weight on his forearms as he thrust into her. Again and again. Bringing her to a fabulous crescendo.

The second time they came together, Randi was on top, loving him as thoroughly as he'd loved her.

"This night's going to kill me," she sighed when she reached completion for the second time in an hour.

"But what a way to go." He lay back, one arm over his head, the other around her as she snuggled into his chest.

She was exhausted but couldn't fall asleep. She didn't want to waste a minute of her time in his bed. He was giving her tonight. She was only prepared to take tonight. She couldn't bear to lose a second of it.

"Shouldn't we cover up?" she asked, glancing at the clock beside his bed.

"Probably, but who wants to move?"

She didn't. And was glad he didn't, either. They'd been lying quietly for several minutes. It was officially *afterward* and he wasn't running off.

Or running her off.

The third time they made love, they were lying on their sides, facing each other. Neither of them above the other, or below. They coupled as partners, looking into each other's eyes.

Randi liked that way best of all. It was a completely intimate expression of give-and-take.

She tried to doze after that. To be content lying in Zack's arms, in his bed. But now that she was sated, thoughts were crowding in on her. And worries returned. Maybe she'd liked Zack's touch just a little too much.

He wanted temporary. Wanted things short and sweet.

They had the sweet part down, but how many times constituted short?

And how many times could she do this without upsetting the well-ordered contentment of her life?

Maybe she shouldn't stay. She was probably risking too much, lingering there, getting cozy in a bed that wasn't hers. That wouldn't ever be hers.

Zack settled in beside her, tucking her more securely into his side. He didn't say anything, but she didn't think he was asleep. His breathing wasn't deep enough.

If Zack was such a caring guy—as his commitment to animals and to his pet-therapy patients attested—why did he refuse even to consider seeing where something between them might lead?

Not that *she* wanted it to lead anywhere. But why didn't he?

She came up with several possibilities—he liked living alone, he liked variety, he didn't like her—all

of which she immediately dismissed. Even if he liked
living alone, she already knew he'd also liked living
with a partner. He'd believed his marriage was near
perfect. That he and Dawn had been a team.

Was that it, then? He'd never gotten over his ex-
wife? Was still in love with her? He seemed like the
kind of guy who would do the forever once-in-a-
lifetime kind of love. Was that why he wasn't willing
to get involved in another relationship? Because he
knew he couldn't? His heart wasn't his to give?

She could understand that, she supposed. Randi
had no intention of risking her own heart, her own
life, to something outside her control. And a full-
blown relationship with Zack would definitely be
that.

But to think he'd just made love to her so…
so…completely, while in love with another woman.

It made sense, though. Went right along with his
aversion to having anything he and Dawn had shared
in his home. When he'd acted so oddly earlier about
his half of the divorce settlement, sidestepping her
question about where his things were, Randi had realized he was hiding something.

"You awake?" she asked him. If she was going
to lie there figuring him out, she might as well get
his confirmation of her conclusions. She might as
well know the truth.

Or risk kidding herself.

Randi couldn't do that. Not about Zack. Not about

anything. Facing facts head-on was the only way she'd gotten through the accident that had robbed her of her dreams.

"Sort of." His voice was only slightly groggy, his fingers trailing back and forth along her ribs.

Half-awake was good enough. "You're still in love with her, aren't you?"

"Hmm?" He paused. And then asked, "In love with who?"

"Your ex-wife."

"Dawn?" His fingers stopped their caresses.

"Yes."

"Not hardly."

"It's okay," she assured him. "I understand. We both know this is nothing more than an interlude."

"I'm not in love with Dawn," he said again. There was nothing drowsy about him now.

"But it's so hard for you to talk about her. You didn't even want to bring anything the two of you had in your home to this house."

"The issues I have with my first marriage have nothing to do with unrequited love for my ex-wife."

He spoke with such conviction she believed him.

"It's a matter of trust, then? Because she was unfaithful to you?"

"Partially."

He still held her, their voices soft as they spoke in the dark.

"What else?"

"Hey, why all the questions?" he asked, nudging

her. "You're alone, too—and you intend to stay that way."

"I know."

"You *do* intend to stay that way, don't you?" he asked.

His question sounded discordant in the room where they'd come together so perfectly such a short time before.

"Yes," she finally said. Because he deserved an answer. And because she meant it.

What she and Zack shared was incredible. A dimension of life she'd never expected to experience.

But it was only one dimension. And a temporary one. She was a challenge to him. So far, she'd managed to keep him interested. But eventually he'd tire of the game. Tire of having a woman around who was always so…competitive.

If Zack ever did settle down again, he'd pick a really feminine woman. A woman who spent hours putting on her makeup. Who knew *how* to put on an hour's worth of makeup. Who knew what colors to wear, which ones to stay away from.

Who knew how to be a princess.

All the best guys went for girls like that.

SITTING IN HIS HOME OFFICE on Saturday just before lunch, Will Parsons, the president of Montford University, sighed. Being Randi's oldest brother was hard sometimes. He got most of the responsibility for her welfare. Being the brother she fought with the least was hard, too. It gave everyone an excuse to let that responsibility lie firmly on his shoulders because she might actually listen to him. Loving her so much was hardest of all.

Straightening his shoulders, Will looked at the phone.

He'd been putting this off for most of the morning. And knew that if he showed his face at the lunch table without making the call, Becca would send him right back to his office.

Will slung his jean-clad legs up on his desk, leaning back in his chair, arms folded. He didn't want to be in the office any more that day. He had plans to take his girls, Becca and baby Bethany, into Phoenix. He and Becca were getting Bethany's six-month picture taken. And buying her some new clothes. In return, she was going to accompany her parents to a five-star restaurant for dinner and sleep through a show afterward.

There was no way Will would enjoy any of it if he was worried about Randi. Next to Becca and Bethany, he loved Randi more than anyone else on earth. And she was fragile. More so than she knew.

"Hello?" she answered on the fourth ring.

Thank God she was home. He'd been half-afraid she wouldn't be. And then he'd have to think about where she was.

He wished his mother had left him in blissful ignorance. His feet landed on the floor with a thud as he sat forward, shading his eyes. Why were older brothers the last to know these things?

"Hi, squirt," Will said, reverting, in his concern, to the name he'd given her when she was a baby. He'd been twelve when Randi was born and had spent his entire life looking out for her. Protecting her.

"Hey, Will, what's up?"

She sounded normal. Thank God again.

"Not much. How are you?"

"Fine."

"Good." He had to go about this delicately. Randi was a bit touchy about her privacy.

"How's Bethany?"

"Great," he said, smiling at the collection of pictures on his desk. "Rolling over all the time now. I don't think she's ever going to crawl. Maybe not even walk. She's just going to roll."

Randi laughed. "You just wait, brother. Six months from now you'll wish rolling was all she could do."

Maybe. Probably not.

Will picked up a pencil, flicked it repeatedly against the top folder on his desk. Lunch would be ready soon. "You having a good weekend?"

"It's only Saturday morning, but yes, so far it's been good."

What was that note he heard in her voice? Or was there a note?

"Do anything fun last night?"

She paused. "Why don't you tell me what you think I did, and then I'm going to tell you to mind your own business," she said, her voice no longer relaxed.

Damn. He'd pissed her off.

"Or better yet," she said, "since we both know the drill, why don't we just skip it altogether?"

Why did the family always insist he be the one to call Randi? He couldn't handle her any better than the rest of them, no matter what they said. He was probably just the only sucker who'd agree to do it.

"Someone saw your Jeep outside Zack Foster's house last night."

"We were watching *The Sixth Sense*. You ever see it?"

"No."

"Oh, you should. You and Becca have to rent it first chance you get. But don't watch it until Bethany's asleep. It might upset her."

"She's six months old."

"Yeah, but she's at the impressionable age. You never know what she's taking in."

Will inhaled a deep breath. He stared at Becca's desk across the room. It was a mess, as usual, papers all over it. Thinking of his wife gave him courage.

"Your Jeep was still there at four o'clock this morning."

"What the hell is anyone doing looking at my Jeep at four o'clock in the morning?"

She hadn't denied it. Damn. Randi was far too

innocent to be playing these kinds of games with experienced men like Zack Foster. He wasn't from Shelter Valley. Didn't know how they worked.

But he was damn well going to find out. Will made a mental note to kill the guy.

"The family elected me to call and ask you to invite your friend to dinner tomorrow."

"Thank you, but no."

If Randi had to keep the bastard away from her family, Will really *was* going to kill him.

"Why not?"

"Because I wouldn't wish that experience on my worst enemy."

"Mom's cooking," Will said, pretending he didn't know what she meant. "The food will be great."

"With the family interrogating him, he either won't get a chance to eat it or he won't want to."

"You spent the night with him," Will said. Didn't the girl know how badly she could get hurt? Hadn't he taught her anything?

"Not that it's any of your business, but yes. And might I remind you, Will, that *you're* the one who threw us together in the first place? I didn't want that pet-therapy assignment."

Will, who was comfortable speaking to an entire student body of six thousand, who'd faced down his best friend the previous year for having an illicit affair with a student, who headed up one of the leading universities in the country, couldn't think of a thing to say.

"He wasn't the first, big brother," Randi said, her voice softening with humor.

He didn't want to hear that, either.

"He's the first one here in town," he finally muttered.

"Yeah. So?"

"People talk, Randi, you know that."

"And *you* know I've never given a damn what they say."

It was true; she never had. He'd always admired that about her. Probably came from being in the public eye at such a young age. The press wasn't always kind to young female athletes as successful as Randi had been.

"So you like him a lot, huh?" he asked, then rolled his eyes at how high school he'd sounded. What was it with the women in his life? They could always tie him in knots, make him forget that he was highly intelligent and successful.

"I probably wouldn't have slept with him if I didn't like him," Randi said drolly.

"So why, if you're a couple, won't you bring him to dinner?" he asked, getting back to his original mission. At least as far as the family was concerned. "He'll have to meet us all eventually."

"Who says we're a couple?"

"You spent the night with him."

"Yeah."

"Well…"

"We're just friends, Will," Randi said as though explaining something disappointing to a child.

"You spent the night with him." He'd already said that.

"So we're intimate friends, but that's it."

"Randi, you slept with the man!"

"Don't worry, it won't become a habit."

Will sat straight up, his spine rigid. "If he hurt you—"

Laughing, Randi said, "Down, big brother. Zack wouldn't hurt me even if he hated me, which he doesn't, I'm happy to report."

"You guys seem to be spending a lot of time together," Will said, remembering what else his mother had told him. "You've been Rollerblading more than once."

"Plus, we went to Phoenix for dinner a couple of times, and to see a movie," Randi rattled off. "Oh, and he was at my house one night, too. Someone might have seen him leave at a slightly inappropriate hour."

Will's chin jutted out. He really wanted to deck the bastard.

"So why—"

"Did you ever stop to think that maybe I want things this way?" Randi asked.

Will frowned. He hadn't. No.

When had his baby sister grown up so much?

"Why?" he had to ask. Just trying, at that point,

to understand her. To know what would make her happy.

Because, in the end, her happiness was all he cared about.

"Just between you and me?" she asked, her voice soft, pleading.

"Yes."

"I'm content with my life, you know?" The loneliness in those few words stabbed him.

Couldn't she hear it?

"I've learned to accept what I've got and be happy," she continued. "I'm not willing to risk losing that."

A huge knot formed in his stomach. This was a whole lot worse than a sexual escapade. Or even a broken heart.

His sister, who had more potential than anyone he'd ever met, was condemning herself to a life of loneliness. To a life of unhappiness. To no life at all.

CHAPTER THIRTEEN

WILL COULDN'T LET that happen.

"Without risk, you go nowhere," he said bluntly.

He wasn't telling her anything she didn't already know. Randi defined the word *risk.* It was why, at the age of thirty, she'd already accomplished more in her career than most people did in a lifetime of working.

"I'm happy where I am," she said. But she didn't sound like any kind of happy he'd ever known. "I have no desire to go anywhere else."

"You want to live alone forever?" he asked. He couldn't imagine it. Didn't want to imagine it. Not for her.

Randi didn't answer him. Which was far more telling than anything she might have said.

"What about children?" he persisted. "You love being with Bethany so much, it's obvious you'd thrive with a baby of your own."

"You don't always get what you want out of life," Randi said, her voice flat. "The way to achieve joy in this life or at least peace, which I personally find more valuable, is to find a way to be happy with what you have."

When had her head become filled with such bullshit? And why hadn't he noticed?

"What about *making* things happen? If you don't reach out, you won't get anything at all."

"I dedicated the first twenty-one years of my life to reaching for a dream, Will. And in the space of a thirty-second error made by someone else, it was all gone. Dreams are for kids who still have the energy to fight for them."

"I think Bethany is proof that you're wrong about that."

Randi was silent, clearly unwilling to acknowledge what he'd said. Will and Becca had spent twenty years trying to have a baby. Twenty years anguishing over repeated disappointments. But he'd never stopped hoping—even when they'd finally discovered they were expecting and were then told the risks were too high, Becca was too old, they'd have to terminate the pregnancy. He'd never stopped believing.

And here they were, forty-three years old and the parents of a healthy, perfect, beautiful baby girl.

"Please bring him to dinner," Will finally said, afraid his sister might be getting ready to hang up.

She still didn't say anything.

"You know that if you don't bring him, he's suddenly going to be getting an unusual number of drop-in visits at that clinic of his."

Will would be first in line.

"What time is dinner?" she asked grudgingly.

"One o'clock, out at Mom and Dad's.'' After their father had retired from the cactus-jelly plant outside Shelter Valley, where he'd put his business-management degree to use for more than thirty years, their parents had moved into the desert, about fifteen miles from town. They'd built a house big enough for all the grandkids on a plot of land they'd bought when Will was still in high school.

"Okay, but I'm warning you, Will, if anyone tries to marry us off, I'm out of there."

"I'll warn them."

"You do that."

As hungry as he was for the lunch awaiting him in the kitchen, Will couldn't leave things like that.

But he refused to retract the statements he'd made. He couldn't ignore his worry about her relationship with Zack Foster—or her sense of resignation, her false contentedness.

"How's everything at school?" he asked for want of anything else to say.

"I need money."

"For what?"

"A center for my basketball team."

He knew she was putting a load of pressure on herself about that team.

"You've gone to your alumni association?"

"Of course. And to the community funds, too. There's nothing."

"How much over budget would the scholarship put you?"

"I'm already over. I just requested another pay raise for my coaches."

"They got a raise last year."

"And they still aren't making what the men's coaches make. I have to pay them if I expect highly motivated coaches—and winning teams."

"Have you thought about finding a private source to fund a one-time scholarship?"

"Yes," she said slowly. "Actually, I was wondering about asking Barbara Sharp. What do you think?"

"It's a great idea," he said, relieved to be meeting her on common ground again. "She can easily afford it. She makes healthy contributions every year, anyway. She's openly supportive of women athletes and women's athletics. Besides, it'll look good in the papers."

"You don't think I'm trading on a friendship?" Randi asked.

"I think she'd be hurt if you didn't ask."

They talked for a few more minutes. Randi got all the information he had about the red tape of establishing a privately funded scholarship. By the time they hung up, she was ribbing him again, almost like her old self.

But Will was worried about her. Really worried.

"MY FAMILY KNOWS we slept together."

Zack stood back from his front door Saturday afternoon as Randi pushed by him, sidestepped a barking tail-wagging Sammie and walked into his living room.

Telling Sammie to be quiet and stay, he followed Randi.

"You don't have to worry that I'm going to be haunting this place because I've been here once," she said, standing in the middle of the room, hands on her hips.

And what gorgeous hips they were, too. She was wearing her standard attire—leggings, a T-shirt that came only to her waist. And white running shoes.

"You're welcome to come here any time you want," he said.

That seemed to slow her down for a second. She opened her mouth and closed it again without speaking.

"Now, would you mind repeating that opening line?"

He'd just finished showering after a good long game of hoops with his friend Ben Sanders. Had barely pulled on a pair of jeans when the doorbell rang.

"My family knows we slept together."

That was what he'd thought she said. Zack wished he'd had time to put on a shirt. He felt a bit exposed.

"Your family, as in all four of your brothers?"

"And my mom and dad and probably all my sisters-in-law and maybe even the nieces and nephews who are old enough to understand." Hands still on her hips, she nodded her head for extra emphasis.

Cassie had warned him about this. The small-town gossip that could ferret things out better than the best private detective. And spread them faster than any newspaper. "I'm sorry."

"Because your name's linked to mine? I know. I don't blame you. You're going to be hearing about this for a while, I'm afraid."

"It's not *me* I'm worried about. I'm sorry it's put you in a bad position with your family."

She blinked, focused on him for the first time since she'd come barreling through the door.

"You don't have to be sorry for me," she said, calm for the moment. Her brown eyes were still sparkling, but her body wasn't vibrating quite as much. "I'm not worried about my family. Or the rest of the people in town, for that matter. Folks have been talking about me since I was ten, and what I got in Shelter Valley was nothing compared to what some of the national papers said about me when I started winning national tournaments."

He'd never been interested in golf, but he suddenly regretted that. He'd have liked to see some of those articles.

"They're still going to give you a hard time," he muttered.

"They worry about me," she said, dropping her hands from her hips. "But I've been ignoring their nagging since I was a kid. Trust me, that part doesn't bother me a bit. Which is why I didn't think a little harder before I left my Jeep parked in front of your house last night.''

''So what part does bother you?''

''The problem it's going to be for you. I know that the last thing you want is entanglements.'' She grinned wryly. ''My family's going to drive you away before I have a chance to do it myself.''

''You're telling me I should be prepared for shotguns at my door?'' He wasn't afraid of her family. But he'd prefer not to take on four angry brothers at once.

''No, the best thing for you to do is come to dinner with me tomorrow afternoon.''

He frowned. ''How is us having dinner together going to solve anything?'' Not that dinner with her didn't sound like a damn good idea.

''Dinner tomorrow is at my mother's house. Any and all of the family that can make it will be there. It's kind of an open-invitation weekly thing, just changes houses now and then.''

Dinner with Randi's family. Sounded serious. So why wasn't he running in the opposite direction?

''Our goal is to face all the shotguns at one time rather than having them ambush me here?''

He was only half joking.

''Sort of,'' Randi said, not even half joking. ''If you don't come, they'll be showing up at the clinic to check you out.''

''You're kidding.'' Cassie hadn't been exaggerating about this town or Randi's place in it.

"I wish I was."

"Guess I'm going to dinner." He still wasn't as upset about the idea as he should be.

"I'm really sorry."

"I'm not." He had to wipe that regretful look off her face. "It's a small price to pay for the night we had."

They connected for a second there, remembering the things they'd done to each other during the night, but then she grew serious again.

"They're going to have us married within the year."

He frowned, feigning horror. "Can they do that?"

"I mean it, Zack. They've been trying to get me married since I first found out my golf career was over. And I've given them no hope whatsoever. If they have something like this to work with, they're going to be counting grandchildren."

She seemed so worried Zack was almost insulted. Except that they had an agreement about what was and what wasn't happening. Because of that, he understood her unease.

"Hey," he said, crossing to her, taking hold of her upper arms to draw her closer. "We know what we're about," he told her, looking her directly in the eye. "Right?"

She nodded.

"And no one can make us do anything we don't want to do."

"I know that," she whispered, her eyes still

clouded. "I'm not afraid of them or afraid I'll be forced into something I don't want. I'm afraid they're going to scare you away right when I'm having the time of my life."

The time of her life, huh? Well, that was okay, then.

"You don't have to worry about that. I'm not ready to give up my skating buddy yet."

Last night aside, that was all they were. They were two people who challenged each other, enjoyed each other, stimulated each other's minds. They were friends.

Who'd happened to kiss a time or two.

Her lips were only inches away from his…

Zack had taken possession of them before he could even form the thought. Before he could wonder if maybe this wasn't too much. Too soon.

Before he could figure out how to remain friends while keeping things short and sweet.

RANDI HAD NO IDEA how they'd gone from discussing the commitments they weren't going to make to being naked on his bed. For a relationship that wasn't, they sure were doing things wrong.

She couldn't seem to get enough of Zack, didn't even think about stopping him.

It was as if they hadn't made love in months, maybe even years, as they came together, familiar enough with each other to know what pleased. There was no time for talking or for slow leisurely touches.

It was a desperate meeting of hot and hungry bodies seeking instant satiation.

Sweaty and dazed, Randi lay in his arms afterward. "How many times can we do this before we can't do it anymore?" she asked drowsily.

"I don't think there's a limit on it," he said in a lazy voice.

But there was. There had to be. She sat up.

"I'm serious, Zack."

His brows drew together as he raised his eyes to meet hers. "You want a number?" he asked. She could tell he didn't understand.

She wasn't sure she understood, either. None of this. How could a woman who guarded her life so carefully, who guarded her aloneness so carefully, be lying in this man's bed for the second time in twenty-four hours?

"We've said over and over that neither of us is looking for a relationship, right?"

He was frowning in earnest now. "Right."

"You prefer to keep things short and sweet."

"Right."

"So how many times can we go crazy like this before we have a relationship on our hands?"

He sat up, tossing her the comforter folded along the bottom of the bed to cover herself with and pulling the sheet around his waist at the same time. "I see what you mean," he said. He looked at her, looked away, then brought his eyes back to hers.

"What do you think?" he asked.

"I don't know." And not knowing scared her to death. "You're absolutely certain you don't want to try a relationship?"

"Aren't you?" he countered.

"I think I'm certain." She gave him the truth. "But actions speak louder than words, don't they?"

"Usually."

She nudged his thigh with her toes. "Your actions are speaking, too, you know."

"Yeah, but they aren't saying I want a relationship."

She tried not to feel the blow dealt by his words. There was no reason to react as if he'd said something hurtful. She was still in control; that was what this talk was about. Maintaining the control she was on the verge of losing.

"What are they saying, your actions?"

He studied her face. "Hell if I know."

"Then how do you know what they *aren't* saying?"

It wasn't that she was pushing him to get involved with her. Rather, she was pushing him for understanding, for answers that she didn't have herself— not just for him, but for her, too.

"I know I can't get involved again."

Her heart sank even though it wasn't supposed to. "Why?" she whispered.

Her breath wasn't supposed to catch in her throat, either. Perhaps she should have waited to have this conversation.

Zack got up, found his jeans in the tangle of clothes and covers at the bottom of the bed and slid them on. Randi didn't like the feeling of being the only one undressed, so she pulled on her clothes, too, and then sat down on the end of the bed, waiting.

Crossing to the window, he stood silently for several minutes before he turned back to her. He ran a hand through blond hair tousled from their lovemaking.

"My wife didn't leave me for another man," he finally confessed. The effort seemed to drain him. His blue eyes were dulled, almost lifeless.

"But you said..."

Had he lied to her?

"I said she left me because she was in love with someone else."

Randi nodded. She desperately wanted to know the secrets he guarded so carefully. To jump into his life. To understand.

Zack turned his back to her again, gazing out the window. Randi had a feeling he wasn't seeing whatever was out there.

"What I told you was true," he said with obvious difficulty. "There was someone else. It just wasn't a man."

"Oh." Oh, God.

Randi stared down at the running shoes that had landed at the end of his bed, reached down to put one on. Then the other. She left the laces hanging there, untied. Uneven.

"I never had a clue," he finally said, almost as though speaking to himself. All she could see was his back.

"There's no reason you should have, is there?" Randi asked, her mind reeling. She had a hard enough time dealing with the concept of women loving women, and she'd been around it most of her adult life. But for a man to find out his wife—

He shrugged. "A guy ought to notice when he's not doing it for his wife."

"Women can give pretty convincing imitations."

He turned then, looked at her. "I know for certain you weren't faking a damn thing," he said.

"So?"

"By the same token, I should have known that she was."

"And what good would that have done?"

"All the good in the world! If I'd known there was a problem, I could have taken care of it, been more in tune to her needs, found other ways to please her."

"Surely you don't think you could have affected her sexual preferences," Randi said, aghast as she got an inkling of just how deep-rooted his anguish was. No wonder he didn't want to trust himself to a long-term relationship again.

He felt personally responsible for his wife's choices. Even though he had to know better. Suddenly, so many things became clear. A man who half believed he'd failed to satisfy his wife—and feared that failure was why she'd sought the embrace of a woman—would certainly hesitate to take a second chance.

"Zack, it's true there are some women who are driven by men to seek the solace of a woman's arms." He stiffened and she hurried on. "But those are abusive men. Those women have had nothing but violence from men and seek women more for the safety of a soft haven, for comfort and gentleness, than because of sexual desire."

He didn't turn around, but his shoulders relaxed just a bit, as though he was willing to listen to what she had to say. Willing to find a way out of his private hell if one could be found.

"There are also women who, through no fault of their own or anybody else's, get turned on by women, instead of men." She spoke slowly, carefully. "Because of constraints put on them by social expectations, they often don't acknowledge those feelings. They often try to fit the accepted norm, marry, have families. But the feelings are there, and there's nothing they can do to change them."

He turned around now, his hands in the pockets of his jeans, his eyes blazing with emotion as he waited silently for her to continue.

Randi continued to spout facts she'd gleaned over the years in her attempts to understand some of the women around her. To not only accept their choices without judgment, but to understand them, intellectually if not emotionally.

Zack was listening intently.

"There've even been some scientific studies conducted that give credence to the belief that there's a gay gene, so to speak."

His eyes narrowed. "What kind of studies?"

"One study involved identical twins separated at birth and raised in completely different environments. If one turned out gay, in many cases, so did the other."

Randi wished she'd paid more attention when she'd first read about the studies. Wished she could give him something more concrete.

He stood, gazing out into the afternoon sunshine. The man was proud. And exacting. He wasn't going to let himself off the hook easily.

"Do you do anything different when you're making love with me than you did with her?"

He turned to glare at her. "What kind of question is that?"

She held her ground. "Humor me here. Have you perfected some new technique since Dawn left?"

"Of course not! I don't have a…a set routine."

"You're a fabulous attentive lover, Zack."

His eyes burned into hers. His jaw was clenched, but he remained silent.

"Dawn's preferences were all about her and nothing to do with you," Randi finished softly. "Nothing at all."

CHAPTER FOURTEEN

CASSIE TATE was tired. She'd come in on an early flight from Baltimore that morning, done a surgery at the clinic, seen a couple more patients, and now she wanted nothing more than to go home. She wanted to slide into a bubble bath, her long red curls secured on the top of her head, and have a drink. And if the silence got to be too loud, she could always flip on the Friday-night news on the radio in her bathroom. Or the stereo in the bedroom that was wired into the bathroom, as well.

But before she could do any of this, she had to finish up at the clinic. She hadn't seen Zack in more than a week, and though they'd spoken on the phone almost every day, she didn't feel right about being back in town and not touching base with him. Discussing clinic business, making plans.

He was still in surgery. Cleaning an elderly cat's teeth, Adrienne, their former-Montford-student-turned-receptionist, had said. Cassie could have sat in the outer office, making small talk with Adrienne. Probably should have. But Adrienne had a new baby at home and Cassie just couldn't bear to hear about every first the child was experiencing. First smile. First frown. First time he discovered his fingers.

Another night she'd listen. Tonight she was just too tired.

She waited for Zack in his office, sitting in the high-backed chair behind his desk, twirling around in it as she surveyed the room. No pictures or posters on the walls. The books so neatly on the shelves, moved from his office at the clinic in Phoenix. The files so orderly on his desk. She had a television in her office. Maybe she should have waited there. Except then she might miss him.

She'd been wondering all week how he was doing. She'd known Zack for years, long before Dawn had been in the picture, and she was worried about him. He'd been the brother she'd never had since the first day she'd met him at college. She'd been scared and alone....

There was one thing she knew for certain: the man was too bighearted, too generous, to spend the rest of his life sharing his home only with animals.

Cassie knew how utterly lonely that kind of life was.

"Hey, Cass, I heard you were back!" Zack's voice saved her from thoughts that were getting morose.

She whirled around in the chair, smiling as she saw him in the doorway. His blond hair was tousled, his lab coat wrinkled—and he was obviously delighted to see her.

"How was your trip?" he asked.

"Good. Productive. We've got most of the East Coast colleges on board for accredited classes in pet therapy as part of their veterinary science degree."

"Your accomplishments continue to be amazing."

Cassie shrugged. It was easy to accomplish things when you didn't have to answer to anyone else. Her time was completely her own, which allowed her to do so much more than most career people, who also had families.

In some ways she was really very lucky. She spent almost every waking moment doing something she loved.

"How're *you* doing?" she asked.

Taking the chair opposite his desk, Zack filled her in on clinic business for the next forty-five minutes. From supplies and vendors, to personnel and patients, he gave her as thorough a rundown as he always did, wanting to ensure that she was still in control in spite of all her time on the road.

That was just like Zack, to consider her feelings, assess them so accurately. She needed to feel in control at the clinic. It was her life.

He told her about the pet-therapy visit scheduled for next Thursday afternoon. And about an electrical outage that had shut them down for a couple of hours the day before.

"You still skating?" she asked when he finally ran out of things to report. She'd been thinking about him and Randi Parsons all week. Worrying that Zack was going to get hurt all over again.

He'd never survive a second breakup. Hell, she wasn't even certain he'd survived the first, though his interest in Randi was at least giving her hope in that direction.

"At least a couple of times a week," he said, taking sudden interest in the files on his desk. He pulled them onto his lap, started perusing them.

If he'd been preparing to see patients, she'd have understood. But he was done for the day. Zack had no real need to see those files.

"With Randi?"

"Yes."

"So you ignored my warning."

She didn't know why she was surprised. Zack had always been one to listen and then do whatever he'd decided to do, anyway. But she'd hoped, in this case, that she'd convinced him.

"I met the family on Sunday," he said, tapping the folders against his knee. "Nice folks."

"You met her family." This was far more serious than Cassie had imagined. Could it also be good news?

He nodded.

"She took you to her parents' place for Sunday dinner." Randi wasn't known for bringing people home with her. There used to be articles in the paper about how closely she guarded her privacy, how she was generous with her time, with her money, but not with her family.

"Don't get that look, Cass. It wasn't exactly Randi's idea."

Cassie's heart sank. "What happened?" she asked. When he looked back at the folders, she said, "You might as well tell me. I'm bound to hear it from somebody else, anyway."

"I learned *that* lesson."

"I know it's not what you're used to, but that's Shelter Valley. And I did warn you. In this town we count on each other to take care of our own." It gave her a certain measure of peace, actually, to be living in a town where people cared.

Zack frowned. "You worried that my actions are somehow going to reflect on you? Everyone knows you're the reason I'm here."

"Don't be ridiculous," she scoffed. "I'm worried that you're going to get hurt."

"Stop mothering, Cassandra," he said with a chuckle. "I'm a big boy. And I have no intention of getting hurt."

"Tell me how it happened that Randi took you home for dinner."

"Her car was seen outside my house all night last Friday. Will called her the next day and the gist of it was, either I come to dinner and let them all have a go at me, or the Parsons brothers would be appearing at the clinic one by one."

And that news was a fitting end to this day. Hand over her eyes, Cassie lowered her head, then raised it again, looking at Zack.

"So how was dinner?" Did she even want to know?

"Great. We had chicken and dumplings. Mrs. Parsons is a wonderful cook."

"Zack!"

He grinned. "Dinner was fine. Everyone was pleasant, at least on the surface. I can't guarantee some of the guys weren't hiding shotguns, but no one pulled one on me."

Cassie smiled. "It's a good thing, because even you would have a tough time taking on four brothers bent on avenging their sister's honor."

Sitting back, an ankle across his other knee, Zack shook his head. "Randi's got them under her thumb. All it would've taken was a look from her and I'd have been set free."

"Weren't you even a little intimidated?" Cassie asked, avidly curious. She wished she'd been there to see Zack confronting the entire Parsons tribe. Zack, who'd been an only kid in a very lonely household.

"No," he said. "I'll admit to being a bit uncomfortable at first, but they're really very nice people and they set out to put me at ease. I'm fairly certain Randi read them the riot act before I got there."

"You didn't arrive with her?"

"I had an emergency here at the clinic and I didn't get out there until dinner was already on the table."

"What happened here?" Cassie asked, frowning. He hadn't said anything about an emergency.

"That was Mrs. Warner's cat—I told you about him," he said.

He was right; he had. Mrs. Warner's nine-year-old cat had been attacked by a coyote, and Zack had told her how, despite everything he'd done, he'd been unable to save him. What he hadn't told her was that he'd come in on his one day off to deal with the situation.

She sat back, folded her hands across her ribs. "How serious is this thing between you and Randi?"

"We're just friends."

"You're sleeping together, Zack."

"Not on a regular basis."

"Which is how often?"

"Not that it's any of your business," he said, looking at her pointedly, "but we really don't have a relationship in that sense. We're enjoying each other's company immensely, but neither of us wants complications."

Damn. And she'd been hoping for so much more.

Of course, because it was Randi, she was a little relieved, too. Her family's protectiveness could become overbearing to someone like Zack. And did he know that one of Randi's closest friends was Dawn's new lover?

Cassie doubted it.

"And what does her family think is going on?" Cassie asked.

Zack shrugged. "There wasn't one word said about marriage."

"Come on, Zack. The Parsonses are good people. They aren't going to take it lightly if you toy with Randi and then go your merry way."

"Let's get one thing straight." He sat forward, his eyes serious. "I do not toy with women, period."

"I know." She couldn't meet his gaze. "I'm sorry."

"In any case, both Randi and I made it completely clear to them that we enjoy each other's company. A lot. But that neither of us wants anything more than that. They seemed a bit disappointed, but were okay about the whole thing. You're right. They're good people. I like them."

"You mind if I take myself out of your business and back where I belong?" Cassie asked, looking up.

"You have my permission to take yourself wherever you please," Zack said, giving her the warm smile that never failed to make her feel better. "In my business or out of it, you're always welcome. You know that."

"You're a good friend, Zack Foster," Cassie said, wishing, just for a second, that there was something permanent between him and Randi, in spite of Randi's connections. She'd like nothing better than to see him married and having a family. Unless it was married and having a family right there in Shelter Valley. With Randi he might have had both.

"You're a good friend, too, Cassandra Tate," he told her. "The best. I'm glad you're home."

''Me, too,'' she said. The surprising thing was, she meant it.

THEY SLEPT TOGETHER again.

He'd promised himself that he'd keep his hands off Randi. Telling her about Dawn had confirmed to him that he wasn't going to get involved again. Not on any kind of long-term or even semipermanent basis.

There was just one problem. He couldn't keep his hands off Randi.

They'd been skating Tuesday night, a safe, untempting and very public activity. They'd talked about her assistant athletic director who was pregnant, about one of his canine patients who was ready to deliver any day now. They'd talked about paying bills and he'd asked about the scholarship for her basketball player. Her brother Will was helping her get private funding, but her possible source was out of state for the next couple of weeks. And she couldn't say who she was approaching in case the donor preferred to remain anonymous. Zack could understand that and felt foolish for having asked.

Randi had a tendency to do that to him, keep him a little off balance and on the edge. Being with her was a challenge in many ways, and Zack had always thrived on a good challenge.

They'd talked about the morning news, her family and about their joint pet-therapy project.

Afterward he'd simply stopped at her place long

enough for a drink of water and then, in spite a week and two days of success, he'd buckled without a single hesitation. He'd had his drink, set his glass down, picked her up and carried her to her bedroom as though he had every right to do so.

This time, he'd said goodbye, very thoroughly, before he slipped out in the middle of the night.

And here it was, less than twenty-four hours later, the occasion of their next pet-therapy visit. He was like a randy teenager waiting for her to show up. Waiting to see her lithe gait, her sexy smile. Waiting for the look that was only for him.

So maybe they *could* be sleeping buddies. No expectations. No entanglements. Two households. Two separate lives. Just sharing a bed. A bit untraditional, but then, Randi was untraditional, and if it made them happy…

"Is Coach Parsons coming?" Renee asked.

She was playing with Angel, her canine companion, and had been engaging Valerie, her mostly silent human partner, in a one-way conversation.

"She'll be here," Zack said. Running, belligerent, working up the strength to pretend she wasn't nervous driving with a van full of dogs—all two of them—but she'd be there. He now understood why she had a closet full of running shoes. She needed them to keep up with herself.

The guys were kicking a couple of hacky sacks back and forth in the mostly deserted parking lot. Their dogs were in the school van he'd be driving,

their heads hanging out the open windows. Beth and
Marisa were petting Bozo, a yellow Lab-shepherd
mix, and talking as though they were the only two
people in the world.

Zack was growing fond of all of them. They were
great kids, giving up afternoons when they could be
in the student union, out with friends, studying,
sleeping in their dorms and any number of other
things, in order to make some older people's day a
little brighter.

Turning to see if maybe Randi was coming from
the opposite direction, Zack told Sammie to be patient just a few minutes longer.

With or without the Montford Pet Therapy Club,
Zack would be making these visits. But he'd never
be able to see the number of people they all saw
together, nor see them as often.

"Whew, sorry I'm late," Randi said from behind
him. Her face was flushed and she was out of breath.
"The tennis match ran over, and we were winning.
I lost track of time."

"No problem," Zack said, his world right, now
that she was here. "The people we're going to see
don't have anywhere else they have to be…"

Knowing the routine, the kids piled out of the vans
when they arrived in Phoenix at yet a third nursing
home, got their assignments and took off in groups
of three. Two students and a dog.

Which left Zack and Randi with Sammie. Again.

"Let's go, shall we?" Zack asked, clicking Sammie's leash onto her collar.

"I'm ready when you are."

She walked on the opposite side of him, away from Sammie, but there wasn't any holding her back. He might not have sold Randi on dogs yet, but she was definitely becoming a convert to pet-therapy.

"Why is it you're afraid of dogs?" Zack asked casually as they walked down a hallway on their way to visit an old blind man, who was another of Zack's favorite people.

"I was bitten by one when I was two," Randi said.

"So, because a bad father beats his kids, are you afraid of all dads?"

"No," she said aggressively.

"Then—"

"Point taken, Foster. Now lay off."

Grinning, Zack figured he was making progress.

"Hey, Leonard," Zack said as they entered the man's room. "Ready for your shower?"

"I thought you guys'd never get here." The man's gravelly voice boomed from the corner of the room. "I need a shower, man!"

Zack walked Sammie over to him and wrapped the dog's leash tightly around the old man's hand. "We'll have that taken care of in no time," he said.

Taking Leonard's other hand to guide him, Zack led his little entourage out the door and down the hall. Randi followed, watching Sammie with an eagle eye, as though prepared to leap forward and save the old man if the dog made one wrong move. "O, ye of little faith," he muttered to himself. Still, it *was* rather amusing.

At the door marked "shower," Zack stopped, opened it, let go of Leonard's hand and watched as Sammie and the man disappeared, the door closing behind them.

"She's not a seeing-eye dog," Randi said, frowning. "Shouldn't you go in there? Or go get some help? I know you think your dog's a genius, Zack, but he could slip in there."

"After he went blind, Leonard's family put him in this home," Zack said, leaning against the wall.

"Zack, didn't you hear me?" Randi asked. She looked around them. "Someone needs to know he's in there alone."

"Shoved him off as though, without eyes, he no longer had ears or a brain or a heart," Zack continued. "And all because he'd become frightened of water as a result of his blindness."

"Well, then—"

"He's still frightened of water," Zack said, wanting her to trust him, trust Sammie. Neither of them would put an old man's life at risk. "Between that and his sense of modesty, the situation seemed hopeless. If anyone tries to get him in the shower, he panics, hits, swears, bites, anything to save himself."

Randi nodded thoughtfully as he spoke.

"Not only does it make life difficult for his caregivers, but it strips him of the little dignity he has left. Can you imagine standing there, completely naked and unable to see a thing, throwing a tantrum you can't control, while some stranger tries to bathe you?"

She swallowed, her eyes moist. "No."

She looked at the door. The room behind it was small. Tiled floor with a drain, a bench and towel rack outside the shower curtain, and a showerhead and soap dish inside. There was no screaming going on. But the faint sounds of running water—and a gravelly baritone singing voice—could be heard.

"It's the oddest thing," Zack said. "We discovered it quite by accident, but Leonard's fine in the shower as long as he has a companion who isn't a threat to his modesty, his dignity. He holds Sammie's leash and he showers just like he did all the years of his life when he could see. The water no longer terrifies him, and he's not humiliated by having someone standing there holding his hand, watching him."

"Really," Randi said, staring at the door.

"Really."

"And Sammie doesn't mind getting wet?"

Zack shook his head, leaning against the wall, feeling good as he watched Randi and listened to a contented old man sing.

"Sammie runs through the sprinklers at home whenever they're on and she can get past me," he told her, grinning. "But she won't get wet in there. Not unless Leonard has a problem. Then she'll bark and let me know he needs help."

"So what happens to Leonard when we're visiting other places?" Randi asked.

She'd said *we*. Said it naturally, without thinking. Life was good.

"He's visited twice a week by dogs from other volunteer programs."

"Oh." Randi nodded in approval. "I'm glad."

He had one hell of a kiss waiting for those lips.

CHAPTER FIFTEEN

RANDI HAD A BIRTHDAY PARTY to attend. And she didn't want to go alone.

She always went to these things alone. Was usually fine going alone; others would be there without companions.

But it was such a long drive home from Phoenix, late at night, when you were alone. Especially if you'd had a glass of wine at the party.

But she'd made the drive a million times, she reminded herself. Liked driving by herself, thrived on the freedom of being out on the open road.

Besides, people would ask questions if she *didn't* go alone. Might even assume things, which would be awkward. Especially later, when she went alone again.

But then, people always assumed stuff. There wasn't anything she could do about it. She'd learned that a long time ago, and later, learned not to care what other people thought. And where was the harm in having them think she had a gorgeous guy—for a while?

The harm would come later, when she was alone

again and they thought she wasn't woman enough to keep her man.

Of course, she didn't care what they thought.

She cared what *she* thought.

What a great time she'd have, introducing Zack to her friends and acquaintances, the crowd she'd grown up with. And later, it would be fun to talk about them. Party postmortem. She'd have someone to tell all the little things to that she wouldn't dare say to anyone else. Such as she was certain Sandra Diamond had had a facelift. And probably a boob job, too. And Tommy Mortimer was having an affair.

Angela Mooney carried little bottles of gin in her purse and doubled her gin and tonics when she thought no one was looking. Richard Lyons was a tightwad. Walter Brown cheated at cards.

She liked the way Lori Ryan laughed. And wasn't Brad Armstrong a great storyteller? Lindsey Miller told the best jokes. And Bruce Miller made the best drinks....

"You trying to lose me?"

Randi turned around, her reverie interrupted as Zack came skating up behind her.

"No, just sprayed my wheels last night like I said I was going to. Apparently you didn't."

"Nope."

Neither of them had done it over the weekend, which had been the original plan.

She actually hadn't seen him at all the previous

weekend. And that was as it should be. They weren't an item.

And because she'd made it through the entire weekend without him, she could be forgiven for their lapse on Tuesday. It didn't mean anything. They'd just have to get used to being together without touching each other.

They were mature adults. They could manage.

She certainly could manage. She'd lived for years without sex. Making it through more than a week this next time shouldn't be much of a challenge.

They hadn't even kissed good-night when they'd returned from pet therapy. Merely said goodbye at their respective cars, went home to their respective homes and lived their respective lives.

They could do this.

"There's a birthday party in Phoenix a week from tomorrow." She glanced behind her for traffic and crossed the road, intending to take a side street that led to Montford. She liked skating around the university with its signs of student life.

"There're probably lots of parties going on," Zack said as he caught up with her.

"Yes, but I got an invitation to this one. One of my good friends, Lindsey Miller, is throwing a surprise fortieth birthday party for her husband, Bruce. Lindsey's a councilwoman in one of the little suburbs of Phoenix, but in her other life, she was a damn good tennis player. They give great parties. Casual. Lots to do. They've got a beautiful pool area set off by a wrought-iron gate, and a separate patio with Ping-Pong and darts, and out farther, a lighted tennis court. It's all wired for sound, the grill's usually going, there's a full wet bar out there..." She sounded like a salesperson. Was she afraid he wouldn't go just because she'd asked him to? That she needed something else to convince him?

She wasn't even sure she *wanted* him there with her.

"Sounds like fun. You going?"

"I'd offend them if I didn't."

Zack skated silently beside her.

"I'd like you to come with me," she began, "if you don't think it would put us over the line into entanglements we don't want. If you're free and want to come, that is."

"I'm free, and I'd be glad to come. Like I said, it sounds like fun."

He wanted to come. Phew.

"I have to warn you, though, there'll be a lot of talk about the old days there," she said. "It won't be the athletes' crowd, but these are still people who knew me back when I was golfing."

"I'd enjoy that, too."

"Really," she said in that way she had of asking for confirmation without asking a question at all.

"I have a feeling I'm missing out on some great stories that might make good blackmail material in the future."

Future, huh? Blackmail material? That was just fine by Randi.

Without any warning, without even looking at him, she called, "Race you," and sped off. They'd just reached the loop they usually raced around.

Randi was in the lead the entire way. At one point, not wanting him to call foul on her head start, she waited for him to catch up and then lit out again.

She won by several squares of sidewalk. Finally. And wasn't the least bit reluctant about gloating.

"You had an advantage," Zack said, pointing to her skates.

"Hey, buddy, you could've taken care of your wheels, too. Simply put, I used my head. You didn't. You had the same weapons, but you didn't take advantage of them. I win."

"Congratulations. Now get your butt home before I forget that it's off-limits."

She headed out in front of him, sensing him behind her, and eventually slowed until they were gliding side by side down a shady tree-lined street. It was dinnertime and no one was around, giving the impression that they were in a world of their own.

"Hey, Zack?"

"Yeah?"

"How much longer do you think we can keep this up? Telling ourselves each time we sleep together that it's the last?"

He was silent for a while, skating beside her, her

question hanging between them. The air was cool on her face. Sweat was dripping down her back.

"Does it matter?"

"I'd rather fall into the problem head-on than get there by default," Randi said, frowning.

They had a problem. She needed to deal with it even if he didn't.

"Mind explaining that?"

"I'm just wondering if it might not be less damaging to *choose* to have a relationship, to feel we had some say in the matter, rather than losing control enough times to be having a relationship without ever choosing it."

"Or we can continue to try to control ourselves."

She looked over at him, caught his eye. "And you honestly think we have a hope in hell of being successful? After Tuesday?"

She could see that he didn't. And see, too, that he wasn't happy about the situation.

"What have we got to lose, Zack?" she asked, taking his hand as they coasted to a stop at a deserted street corner. "If we do this and it doesn't work, we're no worse off than if we'd never tried at all."

"Aren't we?" He searched her face. "You aren't hurt now, but you could be."

And so could he.

"You think you could walk away now, never see me again and not care?" she asked.

"No."

"Me, neither. Which means I stand to get hurt either way."

"But if we try," he said slowly, "we have a chance at having it all."

Randi nodded. "Will told me not too long ago that if you don't reach out, you never get anything. He was right."

Zack started to skate again, still holding her hand. "I must say, there's something pretty damn tempting about knowing we can make love any time we want," he said after a moment. "How big a chance are you proposing we take?"

"Not big." Randi wasn't even sure she was ready to take any chance at all. She just didn't know of any other intelligent solution.

Pretending not to be lovers wasn't cutting it.

"I'm just winging it here," she continued, "but one thing's for sure, I don't want any promises. And I can't make any."

It was probably the single most important conversation she'd ever had, and she was having it while skating down the middle of the street.

"Agreed."

"At the same time, I expect fidelity, at least while you're...while we're..."

"Sleeping together?"

Desire shot through her just hearing him say it. "Yeah."

"I expect the same."

"Okay."

"Then we're agreed."

Randi nodded. "I feel we should tell someone," she said, loving the feel of his big hand wrapped around hers. Loving the intimacy of holding hands in the street. "Except I don't know what we'd say."

"I think we've already said it," Zack told her, smiling down at her. "We were just the last ones to listen."

They skated in silence until they were back across town and at the end of her street.

"You sure you're okay with this?" she asked him.

"Right now all I can think about is that I'm going to be making love to you in about five minutes. And that I'm going to do it again tomorrow and the day after that."

Warmth pooled in her belly as she skated the rest of the way with him, each glide taking them closer to her house, her bedroom, her bed. And tonight, when they made love, they'd be doing so with their minds first—bacause they'd *decided* this—not just with overeager bodies.

There was something incredibly sexy about that.

But as she coasted to a stop at her front door, took off her wrist guards and pulled out her key, Randi wasn't thinking only about sex. She was suddenly overwhelmed with the fear that she was risking too much.

This was her home. Her haven. Her safety net. The one place where the world—and its inherent pain—

never gained entry. The one place where she was in complete control.

WAITING FOR HIS NEXT PATIENT, Zack wandered out to the reception area at the clinic on Tuesday, his thoughts on the upcoming party. He was looking forward to meeting people who'd known Randi in her other life. He'd had a rough moment when he'd thought Barbara Sharp might be there, but dismissed his concern. She'd said it wasn't really an athletes' party. Besides, he didn't think Randi knew Barbara.

Looking out the front door, he saw his buddy, Ben Sanders, coming up the walk. Zack's patient apparently wasn't going to show up, and Zack was delighted to see Ben. Now that Ben was married and had his little girl living with him, Zack hardly saw him anymore.

"What's up?" Zack asked after the greetings were over. "You aren't having problems with Buddy, are you?"

Buddy was the dog Zack had given Ben on Ben's second day in Shelter Valley. It was the day the two of them had met.

"Nope. I actually—" Ben looked over Zack's shoulder to the empty hallway beyond "—came hoping you'd be able to introduce me to Cassie."

"I think she's in one of the examining rooms right now, but if you'd like to come back and wait, I'll be happy to grab her when she's through."

Checking his watch, Ben nodded. "I've got an

hour before my next class. I'll wait if you're sure I'm not holding you up.''

Telling Ben about his no-show, Zack gave the younger man an impromptu tour of the clinic's facilities.

''You guys ever think about doing any boarding?'' Ben asked, glancing around the spacious back room. Currently about a quarter of the room was in use, storing supplies. The rest just got swept once a month.

''We've talked about it,'' Zack said. ''We'd like to keep a couple of dogs trained for therapy right here.''

A dog lover, Ben asked a lot of questions about almost every aspect of animal health before they returned to Zack's office.

''So you're finally going to meet Cassie,'' Zack said, pouring Ben a cup of coffee, then helping himself to one, as well. Ben dropped into a chair in front of Zack's desk. Zack leaned against a corner of his desk, legs crossed in front of him.

''The Montfords are having a party for Tory and me at the end of the month. They wanted to give us a wedding reception, but I managed to talk them out of that,'' Ben said. ''Anyway, invitations are being sent out this week and that motivated me to finally get my butt over here. I'd rather have my first meeting with Cassie privately, as opposed to in a room full of partying people.''

Zack nodded. ''She's very special. I think you'll

like her." She was also the ex-wife of Sam Montford, the cousin Ben had yet to meet.

"I have no doubt about that. I'm more concerned
with how she's going to react to my presence. I'm
hoping I won't be a bad reminder of Sam. Lord
knows, I don't want to make things any harder on
her."

Zack didn't want that, either. He'd wondered a
time or two whether Ben's arrival in Shelter Valley
would make a difference to Cassie. He hoped not,
but he couldn't be sure. Until the past September
nobody had even known there was another Montford
heir. Ben was the grandson of a Montford daughter
who'd disappeared, believed to have been killed at
fourteen.

Cassie must have heard by now that Ben was here,
but she'd never mentioned him. And Zack, respect-
ing their long-ago pact never to mention that dev-
astating part of Cassie's life, hadn't asked her about
it. When she needed to talk, he listened. When she
didn't, he left it alone.

He heard a door open down the hall, recognized
Cassie's voice giving instructions to a relieved pet
owner. And then, as one set of footsteps faded toward the reception area, another grew closer. Cassie's office was next to his. She was coming this way.

"Cass?" he called out to her just as she would've
passed by.

"Yeah?" She stopped in the doorway and looked

at Zack before she noticed the man sitting in front of his desk.

As her gaze landed on Ben, she turned white, in sharp contrast to her red hair. Her brown eyes glinted with emotion, and though her mouth opened, not a word came out. Zack hurried toward her, intent on offering support.

And then Ben spoke. "You must be Cassie."

"Ben Sanders, meet Cassandra Tate," Zack said, his hand on Cassie's back as he made the introductions. His partner looked as if she'd seen a ghost.

"Ben." Cassie nodded her head, obviously speaking with difficulty. Zack admired the way she'd found her composure, clung to it. "So...we finally meet."

Ben inclined his head, but raised it again almost immediately, his eyes taking in every detail. Cassie made an impressive sight, her slim body curved in all the right places, her striking hair and flawless skin, the intelligence in her eyes. Her clothes, what could be seen of them, were designer-quality and fit her well. And her lab coat lent a further impression of competence, of stature and success.

"You look like Sam," she said. The words seemed to catch in her throat.

Ben withstood her stare with compassion, allowing her whatever time she needed.

"Not your eyes," she went on. "His were green. But the resemblance around your nose and mouth is uncanny."

At least she had her color back. Zack relaxed a bit, dropping his hand from Cassie's back.

"His mother said the same thing," Ben said with an embarrassed grin. "The rest of my coloring comes from my Indian ancestors."

They made small talk then. Cassie asked how Ben was settling in, listened attentively when he told her about his school plans, asked about Ben's new wife and the daughter he was in the process of adopting. Ben asked about Cassie, too. About her travels. Her pet-therapy program. A paper she'd written that the Montfords had given him to read.

"Your aunt and uncle are really wonderful people," she told Ben, her eyes filled with the sadness that had been so familiar to Zack in the early days that he'd known her.

"They tell me you're still in frequent touch with them," Ben said.

Cassie shrugged. "They've been like family to me my whole life. Something like that doesn't just stop because of a…a divorce."

"So you'll be at the party they're having at the end of the month?" Ben asked. "I'd like Tory to meet you."

"I have to be there," Cassie said. "I'm doing the desserts."

"Cassie makes fabulous desserts," Zack interjected.

Ben stood, slinging his backpack onto his shoulder. "My wife's friend, Phyllis Langford, is eager to meet you, too," he said. "She's a psych professor at the U and very interested in the pet therapy you're doing."

"I'll look forward to speaking with her," Cassie said. "As a matter of fact, she might find herself drafted. I have a couple of challenging cases I could use some input on...."

Ben and Cassie talked for several more minutes before saying goodbye. As Zack listened, he felt the immediate bond between these two people—and suddenly thought of Randi. Of their decision to be a couple...of sorts. Of her family. And all the friends he'd be meeting at that birthday party later this week.

He felt that same kind of bond.

Life was good.

RANDI DIDN'T GET nervous often. Playing professional sports, especially at such a young age—and being a woman in professional sports—required nerves of steel. She had them.

Which didn't explain why, walking up to the Millers' imposing front door, her stomach was fluttering and she almost giggled for no reason at all.

Giggled. Randi didn't giggle. Found it extremely irritating, in fact. For that matter, she was finding herself rather irritating at the moment. This was just a party. She'd been to more of them than she could count. She'd even brought Sean to some when they were together.

But she hadn't been in love with Sean.

Randi stumbled, almost dropping the bottle of wine and the gift bag she was carrying.

"You okay?" Zack murmured, slipping an arm around her waist.

"Fine."

She wasn't in love. She was not. It was not a good idea. She hadn't made that decision. She just plain wasn't going to go there. Period.

"You looking forward to the evening?" he asked. *He* certainly appeared to be. His face was relaxed, smiling.

He looked great in off-white shorts, a black polo shirt and black leather sandals. With his blond hair, blue eyes and toned body, he could have walked right off a Hollywood movie set.

"Yeah." She answered Zack's question with her mind only half-focused on what she was saying. "It'll be good to see my friends again. It's been a few months since I've gone to any of these events."

And she was going to be walking in on the arm of Adonis. She'd dressed up for the occasion. Bought herself a new pair of tennis-style shorts. Black ones. And a silky white blouse that tied at the waist. She hadn't been able to make herself buy the black sandals with heels that the salesgirl had told her would finish off the outfit. But she'd compromised with a new pair of dressy flat sandals. She was even carrying a small purse, rather than cramming things into her pockets or leaving them in the console of the car as she usually did.

And she'd put on some makeup. Not a lot. But enough to make her feel like a princess going to the ball.

CHAPTER SIXTEEN

LINDSEY GREETED THEM at the door, looking beautiful in a black designer swimsuit with black lace inlays and a matching skirt. She seemed genuinely glad to meet Zack, and pulled them into the middle of the fray immediately. There had to be at least seventy-five people milling around the huge backyard and around the downstairs of the house.

Within minutes Bruce had put drinks in their hands and Zack had been dragged off to be the fourth in a game of doubles table tennis.

"You've done it again, Randi," Lori Ryan said. Lori was married to Billy Ryan, a golf pro at one of the premier clubs in Phoenix. He'd been Randi's coach a long time ago. Billy was currently standing across the Ping-Pong table from Zack.

"Done what?"

"Gone straight to the top. That man's gorgeous. He has a great ass." She laughed lightly. "Oh, and the warmest eyes I've ever seen."

"You noticed, huh?" Randi asked, making a long slow perusal of Zack's backside. It was hers for the looking now. Had been, officially, for a week and one day.

"I don't think there's a woman here who hasn't noticed," Lori drawled.

Laughing, Randi shared an amused glance with her friend. She'd always liked Lori. Younger than her husband by about ten years, she had the body and face of a model, and the heart of Florence Nightingale. She'd helped heal a lot of hurts over the years. Including Randi's.

"So, tell me," Lori said, guiding Randi to a couple of lawn chairs within eyesight of the fiercely competitive table-tennis game, yet private enough to allow for personal conversation. "Does his being here mean what I hope it does?"

Randi set the glass of wine she'd been carrying on the little white table placed between the two chairs. "It's too soon to be sure of anything," Randi said, dying to confide in the woman who'd nursed her through some hellish nights that first year after her accident. Yet afraid to mention the fragile thread that was spinning itself between, around and through her and Zack.

"You care about him," Lori said.

Randi couldn't lie to the older woman. Had almost stopped lying to herself. "Yeah," she said.

"You love him."

Randi let the words go unanswered. It was clear from the way Lori studied her, eyebrows raised, that her silence was telling.

Watching Zack, she saw him make a shot that was

impossible to return. It made her itch to be on the other side of that table, taking him on.

He'd probably win, but she'd have a hell of a time making him work for it. And if they played often enough, she'd get lucky eventually.

Maybe she should buy a Ping-Pong table. There was plenty of room on her back patio. And just think what else they could do with it...

"He obviously cares about you, as well," Lori said, pulling Randi back from her X-rated fantasies. She discovered that Lori was watching Zack, too.

"It's almost imperceptible, but do you notice the way he keeps checking to make sure he knows where you are? Even while he's holding his own in that life-and-death game they've got going on over there."

Randi smiled, warmed by Lori's observation. She *had* noticed, but it was nice to have confirmation that she wasn't just imagining things.

"We're still in the very early stages," she felt compelled to tell her friend. She didn't want to give Lori false impressions.

"Honey, I'm just thrilled to see you in any stage at all." Lori took a sip of her scotch. "It's been ten years since that damned accident, and I was beginning to think you'd died in that Florida hospital, after all. Emotionally speaking, that is."

The words hit Randi hard. Was that what she'd done? Let the accident kill parts of her that really mattered? Because while it had certainly killed a big part of her—her golf career—there was more to her than that, wasn't there? She had a successful new profession, her family, lots of friends...

"Just because I choose to live alone doesn't mean I'm not very much alive," she said with defensiveness born of fear.

She'd thought she handled the aftermath of her dead career remarkably well. That she'd adjusted completely.

That she was happy. Or at least content.

"It was more than your just wanting to live alone," Lori said bluntly. Lori had a certain right to speak to her this way. After the accident, Randi had been so busy putting on a cheerful face for her family, for everyone at home, because they were all so devastated for her, that it had fallen to her coach's wife to see what Randi was really suffering.

"I made it through the first time I had my dreams snatched away," Randi said, her voice hard. "I'm not sure I'd make it a second time." She took a sip of her wine. And then another.

"So why's he here?" Lori asked as bluntly as before.

Randi glanced at Zack, then at Lori. "I'm not sure," she answered honestly. "I don't know why he's in my life at all, except that since the day I met him, I can't get him out. Out of my head, I mean..." She stared down at her glass.

"Out of your heart?"

Randi forced herself to look up again. "Maybe."

"Does he know any of this?"

Randi nodded. "He's got his own plateful of insecurities to deal with, and he isn't any more sure than I am about embarking on something that might not last."

Lori smiled sadly. "You two make quite a pair."

"I know. But at least we understand each other."

The game of table tennis ended and while Zack, a member of the winning twosome, was challenged by his partner, Brad Armstrong, to a game of darts, Billy came over to join his wife and his former protégée.

"Couldn't you have left that one at home?" he groused, jerking his thumb at Zack. His voice was gravelly with age and with years of working outside in the desert sunshine and the unpredictable dust storms.

"I could've, but then how would I have made your life miserable?" Randi quipped.

"You did enough of that when you were fifteen, Miranda, always arguing with me about every damn swing."

"You were a hard man to please."

"You were too good not to give you my best. And, being good, sometimes you were a little too cocky."

"And too stubborn," Randi had to admit.

"Ah, no, my dear," Lori interjected, smiling between the two of them. "That stubbornness is what kept you giving your all. It's what took you to the top. And saved you when everything toppled."

"Probably had something to do with that basketball team of yours winning the title last season, too,'' Billy said.

Maybe.

Randi couldn't help wondering if that stubbornness would also be there to keep her and Zack together for the long haul. Dared she hope she had what it took to hold him? Dared she hope for a real future? Could she hang on until it arrived?

It was another hour before she and Zack had any time together long enough for a conversation. They were huddled by a pillar on the patio, sharing what was left of Randi's second glass of wine, as she filled him in on bits of gossip and observation about the people around them.

Angela Mooney caught her eye and waved, pointing at Zack with her half-full glass of gin and giving Randi a thumbs-up.

''That's Angela,'' Randi told Zack, smiling before she turned toward Zack again. ''Her family owns a chain of sporting-goods stores, and she was always hanging around the big events when we were younger. She married an ex-basketball player and has a couple of kids, neither of whom has any athletic ability at all. Every time she comes to one of these things, she makes a big production of ordering gin and tonic with only half a shot of gin. Like we all don't know she carries little bottles of it in her purse and dumps in a couple more shots.''

''She's an alcoholic?'' Zack asked, glancing over

Randi's shoulder at the pretty though overdressed woman.

"Probably just a party drunk," Randi said. "Her husband's inside with Walt Brown playing poker. His passion. I think she spends a lot of time alone."

"That's a sha— Shiittt."

The change in Zack was so instantaneous it was frightening. One second he was sympathizing with a lonely woman, and the next his entire body had gone rigid, his face harsh.

"What?" Randi asked, her heart thumping. Was he in pain? Having some kind of attack?

He was staring over her head. He hadn't moved.

Randi turned to look, wondering what could have caused such a reaction. All she saw over there, by the corner of the pool, were a couple of lawn chairs and a table. Some landscaping. And her friend Barbara with a woman Randi didn't recognize.

Must be Barbara's new lover, Randi thought.

She hadn't seen Barbara, hadn't even realized she was at the party. She'd figured her friend must not have made it back to Phoenix in time. Whenever they attended these things, they usually spent a while chatting, catching up on news. But that was before Barbara had a companion.

She was glad to see Barbara, not only because she'd missed her these past few months, but because she'd been waiting for her to get back to town so they could discuss possible scholarship funding. She was also a little curious to meet Barbara's friend.

Barbara usually didn't bring her around, choosing to keep her private life private.

But all of that would have to wait. Zack was starting to look really ill.

"Maybe you'd better sit down," Randi said, tugging at his arm. He didn't even seem to notice.

"Please, Zack, tell me what's wrong," she begged. He was scaring her. His eyes, when he glanced down at her—almost as though he'd forgotten she was there—were lifeless. Cold.

"Nothing's wrong," he said eventually. Shaking his head, he took her arm and led her back toward the bar. "Come on, let's get a drink."

He seemed steady enough on his feet. If anything, there seemed to be more energy than usual emanating from him.

Confused, worried, Randi allowed herself to be led. She waited as Zack ordered two more glasses of wine, handed her one and downed the other in a couple of swallows.

"Tell me what's wrong," Randi said, her voice brooking no refusal.

"Nothing's wrong." He smiled at her, his eyes looking right inside her, and Randi began to feel better. She wasn't convinced he was being completely straight with her, but she was extremely relieved to have him back in the same world.

He asked for another glass of wine, and her worry returned. To the best of her knowledge, Zack wasn't much of a drinker. And he was driving, besides.

She'd never known him to have more than one glass when he was driving.

Randi pulled him over beside an orange tree at the edge of the yard. "What happened back there?" she asked.

"Nothing." And when her face stiffened, he added, "I thought I saw someone I knew." He set his untouched wineglass on a tray of dirty dishes.

Lori and Billy joined them shortly after that, and when Billy asked Zack for a rematch at the Ping-Pong table, Zack agreed immediately. His game wasn't quite on, he seemed distracted, but he still played hard, laughed with the rest of them and appeared to be feeling healthy, if nothing else.

Though the knot in her stomach wasn't completely gone, Randi started to relax. She'd been terrified for a minute there, thinking he might be having a heart attack.

She might not believe in forever, but she wasn't ready to lose Zack yet.

Randi didn't see Barbara again until after dinner. It was so odd that Barbara hadn't sought her out. Hadn't been anywhere around. What with Zack's behavior earlier, the night was taking on a surreal, unpredictable quality.

Surely Barbara wasn't feeling awkward because of the recent change in her circumstances. She knew that Randi had never, for one second, thought any less of her because of her sexual preferences.

Not wanting to miss the chance to talk to her,

afraid Barbara might be getting ready to leave soon, Randi grabbed Zack's hand and hurried over.

"Hey, friend, you avoiding me tonight?" Randi asked, tapping Barbara on the shoulder. She'd been joking—until Barbara turned around, and Randi saw the most unusual combination of emotions running across her face.

Randi hardly noticed Barbara's companion, other than to absentmindedly register that the woman was beautiful. She hardly noticed Zack beside her, frozen again. Her gaze was locked with Barbara's as she tried to read the things her friend's eyes were telling her.

Barbara was sorry. And embarrassed. And... afraid?

Nothing made any sense.

Until Zack opened his mouth.

"Hello, Dawn."

The blood drained from Randi's face as understanding almost knocked her off her feet. This was what Zack had seen earlier. His ex-wife and her new lover.

And the new lover was none other than Randi's friend Barbara.

"Zack." The woman's voice trembled.

Randi's eyes flew to her, this woman who'd landed Zack with a world of insecurities, taking in her perfect features, her perfect body, the pain and longing on her face.

She still cares about Zack.

White-hot jealousy seared Randi, leaving her weak. And hating herself. She'd never wasted time on jealousy in her life. She'd learned early on to combat the destructive emotion that ruined so many young athletes.

Besides, it was obvious by the way Dawn stood so close to Barbara, as though absorbing strength through shared body heat, where her loyalties lay. Experiencing a chaos of emotions, Randi started to feel sorry for Dawn. The woman had had to make some hard choices. And it was also obvious that while she wasn't in love with Zack, he still meant a lot to her. She must have valued the friendship she'd lost.

Randi stared from one to the other, all of them standing there without speaking.

"I don't believe we've met." Barbara broke the excruciating silence, extending her hand to Zack.

"Oh, sorry. Zack, this is my friend Barbara Sharp," Randi said, as though it was her responsibility to introduce Zack to his ex-wife's lover. "Barbara, my...date, Zack Foster." She stumbled over the words.

She was afraid Zack was going to ignore Barbara's hand. As it was, he left it hanging there far too long to be polite, but eventually he shook it lightly. He barely looked at Barbara. And after an initial glance, didn't seem to see Dawn, either.

His ex-wife stood there silently, clearly stricken.

The muscles in Zack's jaw were twitching. That was the only detectable movement in his entire body.

"Well, we were just getting ready to leave," Barbara said.

Dawn nodded and turned away.

"Uh, yes," Randi said, trying to think quickly. There had to be *something* she should be doing, something to make these moments less traumatic, to lessen their effects.

There were no bad guys here. Just a lot of hurt feelings.

"I'd, uh, like to get together with you some time in the next week, " she blurted as Barbara gave her one last apologetic glance.

For more than a talk about scholarships.

"I'd like that," Barbara said softly. "Call me tomorrow, okay?"

Randi nodded, aware of Zack, unmoving beside her, wishing there was more she could say.

"Gotta go," Barbara whispered. She followed Dawn, who by that point was crying and hurrying out the Millers' front door.

There'd been tears in Barbara's eyes, too.

Randi couldn't remember ever seeing her friend cry.

"I'M SORRY," Randi said.

Zack's soul flooded with remorse. "You have nothing to be sorry about," he muttered, reaching for her hand across the Explorer's console.

They'd been on the road for more than fifteen minutes and these were the first words either had spoken.

"I took you there."

"You had no way of knowing."

"Are you angry?"

He glanced at her. Could see her face by the lights of an oncoming car. Her beautiful brown eyes, filled with compassion, eased the horrible emptiness inside him.

"I don't honestly know how I feel."

She nodded slowly, only her silhouette visible in the returning darkness of the car. Zack welcomed the anonymity.

"But I'm not angry," he added slowly. "It was just such a shock, seeing her. Seeing them."

Somehow it all seemed so much less *real* when he'd never actually met the woman Dawn was living with. He couldn't erase the image of the two of them standing together; they'd never touched and yet he'd sensed their oneness as clearly as if they'd been making out right there on the floor.

The intimacy of their relationship had been evident in their constant awareness of each other, but it had been far more than that. Which was what had really gotten to him. He knew Dawn better than just about anyone else did, and there had been no doubt tonight that she was truly, fully, in love with her companion.

"She's nothing like I expected."

"Barbara?"

"Yeah."

Okay, maybe he *was* a bit angry. Just hearing the woman's name made him burn.

Yet, when he pictured her standing there, a rather small woman, somewhat defenseless and very human, he couldn't hate her. Or blame her.

"You expected a butch, masculine-looking woman, huh?" Randi chanced.

"I guess. But it wasn't just that. I somehow pictured her as hard, unfeeling."

"Barbara's one of the most sensitive women I know. She even battles with social anxiety."

That didn't fit his image of the worldly pushy woman who'd most certainly strong-armed his wife into thinking she was a lesbian—or so he'd believed.

The woman he'd met tonight didn't seem capable of strong-arming anyone into anything.

They rode in silence for a while, Zack's mind awash with conflicting ideas, illogical thoughts. Where in hell did a man put something like this? Nothing in his life had prepared him for a lesbian wife. Ex-wife.

"Are you still coming in?" Randi asked softly when he pulled to a stop outside her house.

They'd been planning to spend the weekend at her place. His stuff was already there. His Rollerblades, with newly sprayed wheels, were beside hers just inside the front door.

"I'd like to," he said, turning off the engine.

"I'd like you to."

He was relieved to hear the words. Which made no more sense than anything else that had happened in the last couple of hours. All he knew for sure was that Randi was a good thing in his life. That she centered him. That, with her help, he could somehow work through this confusion.

He'd planned on making love to her. Taking a bath with her. Having a middle-of-the-night snack—and then making love again.

Now all he wanted was to lie down beside her, hold her in his arms and find some release in sleep.

CHAPTER SEVENTEEN

HE REMEMBERED SOMETHING just as he was drifting off.

"You said you'd call her tomorrow," he murmured in the darkness of Randi's bedroom. She was lying, spoon-fashion, in front of him, clad only in a loose tank top and panties.

"Mm-hm," she replied sleepily. "We're getting together next week."

Zack told himself it didn't matter. He waited a couple of seconds, giving the tension a chance to leave his body.

"I really wish you wouldn't."

Reaching up, Randi switched on the lamp beside her bed, though she kept it to its lowest setting, bathing the room in a soft glow. She turned over, perched on her elbow, and looked at him. "Why ever not?"

The reasons were obvious to him, but she seemed truly perplexed.

"I'd rather not have the two of you talking about Dawn and me."

That hadn't come out exactly as he'd meant. Randi was silent, waiting for him to do better.

"Just doesn't sit right with me to have two women

talking about their current lovers—who happen to be ex-lovers themselves.''

She didn't look as if she understood. And, judging by the defensive angle of her chin, the shadows in her eyes, she wasn't pleased.

''Just for the record,'' she said slowly, ''while of course we'd have to mention this evening and may even try to figure out how to ease some hurts, talking about you and your ex-wife is not the reason for our meeting.''

He didn't like her tone of voice. Mostly because he knew he deserved it.

''What *is* the purpose of the meeting?'' he asked, turning to Randi as he asked the question. She was his ticket to behaving like the decent honorable man he knew himself to be. For some reason, connecting with her made him feel good.

She sat up in bed, leaning against the headboard, pulling a pillow to her chest and cradling it in her arms.

''In the first place,'' she said carefully, ''we're friends. We've been friends since we were kids. Friends get together. Have lunch. Talk. Catch up on all the news since the last time they saw each other.''

Her tone left no room for debate. Zack sat up, too. He'd left his briefs on, but he wouldn't care at that moment if he'd been sitting there stark naked. He couldn't back down on this one.

She'd understand. He just had to find the right words.

"Barbara's been out of town for several weeks," Randi continued before he found them. "And I was busy with the start of the semester before that. Which means we haven't seen each other since I was in Phoenix the week before school started, helping her with her swing. We have a lot to catch up on."

The mere thought of some of the things they had to catch up on twisted his insides. Didn't women talk about their lovers, first and foremost? He couldn't bear the idea of Randi hearing about his ex-wife being with a woman. *That* woman.

She'd understand. He just had to find the right words.

"You said 'in the first place' as though there's a second place," he said, buying himself some time.

"There is. I have some business to discuss with her."

His eyes narrowed. "What kind of business?"

Hugging her pillow tighter, Randi lifted her eyes to his, then looked away. "I'm really not at liberty to say."

He was losing her. He could feel it. *Think, man. Find the words.*

"Could you at least explain why you aren't at liberty to say?" he asked quietly.

She met his gaze again, her eyes holding his for a long moment.

"Please, Randi." He'd wronged her. He knew that. Drawn a line where there shouldn't be one. "My question comes only from an attempt to understand, to step out of my own battered shoes and into yours. I just want to know what you're feeling.''

She continued to assess him silently.

''A year ago,'' he said, ''my wife comes to me and tells me she's leaving me for a woman. And now tonight, just a week after I decide to try again, my lover tells me she has business with this same woman. I can't help but find that not…good news.''

''I shouldn't say anything, because I haven't spoken to Barbara yet and it would almost force her to say yes if word got out, but I'm intending to ask her for the money to fund Susan Farley's scholarship.''

His lover was going to his ex-wife's lover for money.

Zack was man enough to admit being bothered by that. A lot.

''I'll fund the scholarship.''

''What?''

''I'll write you a check in the morning.''

''No!'' she said, her brows drawn in confusion. ''You can't just write me a check….''

''Then I'll follow whatever procedures are necessary. You don't have to ask Barbara Sharp for the money.''

''Where are you going to get that many thousands of dollars?''

He had that much and more if he tapped into the certificates of deposit that were his half of the liquidation of his and Dawn's assets. The CDs that were sitting, untouched, in a safe-deposit box in Phoenix.

"I make good money," he said now. "And I have very little to spend it on. Especially here in Shelter Valley." And then, needing to be completely open with Randi, he told her the rest of it. The air-conditioned storage garage in Phoenix, the safe-deposit box, the money-market account into which his half of the remaining liquid cash had been deposited.

"Dawn and I both made excellent money," he told her. "We had no family to support and no time to travel. And we made some good investments."

Randi looked as if she'd had too many surprises that night for another one to sink in.

"Why would you want to do this?" she asked him slowly. Finding out he could afford it didn't seem to matter to her. Zack admired her for that.

And he knew that this answer was all-important.

"Because I care about you and I want to help you." It was the truth.

But not all of it.

She was well aware of that; he could tell by the way the expression left her face.

"Then why didn't you offer earlier?"

She had him. He should have seen it coming. *Would* have seen it if he'd been thinking with more than half a brain.

"I've mentioned it a couple of times," she added.

There wasn't a damn thing he could say. She was right.

"You didn't want to help me out last week, but this week you do?" she continued.

"I thought you already had another source lined up."

"I do."

"Yes, but—"

"Be honest with me, Zack. You made the offer just so it won't be Barbara Sharp's money I'm using. If it was anyone else, you wouldn't care."

"Yes. That's true." He met her eyes without faltering. "I made the offer because it was Barbara."

"Why?" Her voice begged for understanding. "It's a business deal, pure and simple. What could possibly be threatening about that?"

Nothing. But it was. Illogical, but very real all the same.

"Getting the money from Barbara is a good business move, Zack," she explained, her eyes asking him to understand.

He was trying. It just wasn't getting past the lead feeling in his gut.

"She'd be a successful female athlete supporting female athletes. In case you hadn't noticed, we're the poor stepsister in the sports world. Anytime we can show one of our own successful enough in her sport to be able to dish out loads of cash, we're doing us all good. People take notice of money. And where there's money, attention follows."

It all made sense. And if she'd been talking about any other woman...

"It would also help Barbara's image, which is something she's working on pretty hard at the moment," Randi continued.

Zack backed up a mental step or two. He didn't want to know about Barbara's problems. Her personal goals. He didn't want to get that close to the woman who'd stolen his wife.

"Barbara has always had problems with social anxiety, and as she's gained fame—and fans—over the years, she's pulled more and more into herself. The press isn't kind to her about it. They call her a snob, someone who puts herself above the rest of the world, when that's not the case at all. She's a warm caring woman who has panic attacks when people crowd her."

"Why does she care about her image?" Zack asked, having a hard time being sympathetic. "You've said she's financially set, she's at the top of her field, so what does it matter what the press says?"

"It doesn't," Randi acknowledged. "And if it were me, that would be the end of it. But it bothers Barbara no end. She reads something like that and gets depressed for a week. On the other hand, good press lifts her up, and providing the means for a young girl to get a decent education *and* to pursue her athletic career, would bring Barbara a lot of good press."

"Which would be why she'd agree to do it," Zack

said, somewhat mollified in his dislike of the woman. She was self-serving, not altruistic.

"No, it would not." The words were spoken slowly and very clearly, though he knew Randi was trying to be patient with him. He could hear it in her tone of voice, see it in the expression on her face.

"I'm going to offer her the opportunity for good press. You know, have the university send out a release, and so on. I expect, though—" she shook her head "—that she'll make me leave her name out of it altogether. She'll probably want us to say only that it came from an LPGA golfer. It'll help the women's athletics cause, but not her own."

Which meant Zack couldn't find any valid reason to detest the woman—other than the fact that she'd broken up his marriage.

Still, that was a damn good reason, wasn't it? He'd lost one woman to Barbara Sharp. Dawn had chosen Barbara over him, and now it seemed Randi was going to do the same thing; just the details were different. With Dawn, it had been Barbara's bed over his. With Randi, it was Barbara's money over his. He had no idea how to explain what he was feeling so Randi could understand, but it made a twisted kind of sense to him.

Right or wrong, it was how he felt. Period.

Zack reached for Randi's hand and held it lightly. "I'm asking you, sincerely, to reconsider this," he said, trying to say with his eyes what he couldn't seem to get out in words.

She squeezed his fingers, her own eyes beseeching, and then let him go. "I can't, Zack."

He stood up slowly, pulled on the shorts he'd taken off earlier, then sank down on the end of the bed. "Nothing's been set in motion yet, has it?" he clarified.

"No."

"Then it's not that you can't, but that you won't."

Another brick wall. Just like the one he'd come up against when he'd asked Dawn what he could do to save their marriage. She'd never given him a chance. What was it about this Sharp woman that garnered such loyalty from those around her?

Zack didn't know, but he wasn't going to spend the rest of his life fighting whatever it was.

"You're wrong," Randi said suddenly, dropping her pillow as she got up and slipped a pair of sweat shorts over her panties.

She looked so damned sexy he ached. It was an ache that would go unassuaged.

He swallowed. "In what way?"

"I don't have a choice. I have to go to Barbara."

There it was again. Running off to Barbara. It was as though she was some sort of witch, casting spells on otherwise sensible women.

"Not you, too," he said, the sting of rejection in his voice. He no longer even knew what he was saying—or feeling. Only that life had become so mixed up he couldn't tell what was real and what wasn't. What mattered and what didn't. And after seeing

Dawn tonight, seeing how peaceful she looked with her companion, he wasn't sure of anything anymore.

And there was the crux of his problem. The axis upon which his entire world had spun was completely and permanently skewed.

NOT YOU, TOO. The words rang in Randi's mind, but she refused to give ear to them, to allow them to affect her. Using a lifetime's worth of skill, she pushed them away, as she'd done with every piece of hurtful press, every bit of snide gossip, every jealous remark she'd been dealt in her life. Sliding her feet slowly into a pair of white running shoes, carefully tying the laces, she said, "I have to go to Barbara for professional reasons, Zack, but for private ones, too."

His head shot up and then he, too, stood, hands on his hips as he faced her. He was so big, so imposing, so frighteningly important to her.

But Randi didn't let anyone intimidate her. She never had. She stood up to challenges and to threats. It was all she knew. The way that had seen her through, kept her on her feet when the storms blew in, and got her standing again whenever she was knocked down.

After looking at her for long silent minutes, he turned to go.

"We're not done yet," Randi said, trying to keep the panic out of her voice.

He turned back to her. Didn't say anything, but he was still there, and that said a lot.

This was hard for him. She understood that. Understood it so well, she could practically feel the confusion and pain she saw in his eyes.

"You're the main reason I have to go to her, Zack," she said.

"I am?"

Randi swallowed. Nodded. Wrapped her arms around her middle, wishing she was wearing more than the translucent white tank top.

"You're never going to be any good to either one of us if you don't learn to have faith in yourself again," she said, hoping he could hear the depth of her feelings for him behind her words. Feelings she'd only discovered that evening, that scared the hell out of her. Feelings she couldn't tell him about. Not with things the way they were now. Not until he'd worked through the insecurities that could destroy him.

"I'll thank you not to analyze my psyche until you're qualified to do so," he said.

Randi choked back the painful lump in her throat. He was so proud. So strong. So much a man in every good sense of the word—if only he could let down his guard enough to recognize that.

"Okay, how's this?" she said. "I need you to have enough faith in me to allow me to go to Barbara and not have it affect us at all."

Standing there, one foot in the room, one foot out the door, Zack looked at her, his eyes sad, resigned.

"I can hardly expect you to understand something I don't understand myself," he said.

"I do understand." Probably better than he did. Which was part of the problem. He was just too caught up in it all; he couldn't see clearly.

"If you understood, you'd take my money just because you're choosing me over her," he said. Then he swore. "And that sounds incredibly selfish."

She smiled sadly. "It does, but I can't blame you for feeling this way."

"You said that giving Barbara the opportunity to fund a scholarship would help her, that it's one of the reasons you want to extend the invitation."

"Right."

"Wanting to help your friend is part of who you are, part of the woman I care about."

Was she getting through to him, then? Randi held her breath as he continued.

"But don't you see that I need your help, too?" He ran a hand through his hair, obviously frustrated. "That, in this instance, you're the only one who *can* help me? There are other ways for Barbara to improve her image. There's no other way for me to know that I come first. Especially where that woman is concerned."

Randi's breath eased painfully out of her lungs. She hadn't gotten through at all.

"I've known Barbara for most of my life, Zack," she said dryly. "If I was going to *choose* her, I'd have done so before now. It's *you* I can't get enough of.''

He waved her declaration away. ''This isn't about sex, it's about one person's influence over another.''

''No, it isn't.'' She shook her head. ''It's about faith, Zack.'' She had to try again, because if she couldn't explain this, there was nothing left to say. ''I need to know that you're secure enough about yourself, and about me, for this not to matter. Because why *should* it matter? If it's not going to affect either one of us—and how could a basketball scholarship do that—then why should it make any difference?''

''I don't know,'' he said, meeting her gaze, his eyes narrowed. ''But it does.''

''Because you still care about Dawn?'' It hurt to even say the words. ''Because you hate Barbara for taking—and keeping—what you want?''

She'd suspected for a while that was part of the answer. Had tried to talk to him about it once before.

''No,'' he said. Not too quickly. And without much emotion. Leaving her in no doubt that at least he knew his own mind. ''I loved Dawn, would have been happy living the rest of my life with her. But that was before I met you.''

His eyes narrowed even more as he looked straight at her, hiding nothing. Randi's heart was pounding.

''What I felt for Dawn was like a cool steady stream, while the feelings you evoke are more like an ocean raging in a storm.''

She wasn't sure if that was a good thing.

But she *was* sure that his feelings for Dawn weren't an issue.

"So what if you'd met me while you were still married to Dawn?"

"I would never have known how you'd make me feel."

"Can you really say that? We sure as hell didn't *choose* to feel any of the things we're feeling."

The conversation was growing odder by the minute. Were they on the verge of breaking up? Or confessing a love neither of them really wanted?

"When I was married, there was a line I didn't cross. A man might look once. But if he's married, or otherwise committed, an honorable man doesn't look twice."

"You'd have stayed away from me," she translated.

He nodded.

"If you'd been married, I could have gotten out of the pet-therapy thing."

"Probably."

Not that it mattered now. She was just stalling. Afraid to let him walk out that door.

"Zack, until you have faith in me, in yourself, in us, we don't have a hope in hell of even getting close to what you and Dawn shared." She forced herself to say what she knew she had to. "I could give in to you now, prove that you come first, but where would that get us? Only as far as the next time your insecurities reared up. I'll spend my whole life proving something that isn't real in the first place if it isn't taken on faith.''

He lowered his head. "You're going to Barbara for the money."

Randi couldn't bear to be so separated from him. She walked over, placed her hands on his chest, taking comfort from the strong beating of his heart. "I'm asking you to let me go," she whispered. "To know, inside yourself, that it isn't going to matter to us if I do." She met and held his gaze, pleading with everything inside her. "I need you to trust me."

"And I need to know that you care enough to understand. That being right or winning isn't what matters as much as putting the other person first."

She stepped back. Beaten. "And are you putting me first?" she asked him quietly.

"What do you call handing over enough money to put a girl through four years at a prestigious college? You win either way, Randi."

"No," she said, shaking her head. "I don't. At the moment, I lose either way. If I take Barbara's money I lose you, and if I give in to you, I lose us. Until you can see that, there's nothing more to say."

His head reeled back. "You mean it?" he asked.

"Yes." She had no choice.

Zack turned and walked out the door without a backward glance.

Standing by her living-room window, watching him drive away, Randi was barely aware of the tears streaming down her face. They felt as though they'd been there forever. Or at least for the ten years they'd been waiting to fall.

Waiting for her to fall.

She was alone. And aching. And scared to death.

CHAPTER EIGHTEEN

INSECURITIES, MY ASS. Zack went for a layup, sank the basket and grabbed his own rebound. In spite of the fact that he was supposed to turn the ball over to Ben.

"What's with you this morning, man?" Ben asked, running the ball down the court. Drops of sweat ran in rivulets down his face and beneath the neck of his T-shirt.

It was Sunday afternoon and they were at the elementary/junior high laying rubber on the deserted concrete court. Zack had survived two days without Randi and he was doing just fine.

He didn't want another woman who wouldn't give him a chance.

Or, at least, he *wouldn't* want her—just as soon as he could exercise her from his system. It was happening. It would happen. And then he'd be whole. And free.

This time he planned to stay that way.

Stealing the ball from Ben halfway up the court, Zack returned it for a jump shot that would have won him a place in the NBA if he'd been that good when the scouts had looked at him during college.

"Time out," Ben gasped, catching up to him. He grabbed the ball from Zack and held it with both hands. "I'm not taking another step on this court until you tell me what the hell is eating you."

"Nothing. I couldn't be better," Zack said, breathing hard. "Don't blame me because you're letting married life make you soft."

"You've got the devil in your eyes, man," Ben told him. "I don't like what's going on with you."

Insecurities, my ass, Zack thought again. He could take on anybody. Anything. He was wiping the floor with a man who was four years younger and probably had more natural talent for basketball than Zack had ever had.

"You're imagining things," Zack insisted.

Ben shot him the ball with a quick flick of both wrists, landing it expertly, and not lightly, against Zack's stomach. "Have it your way," he said. "But until you get things under control, game's over."

Okay, that was fine, too. Zack had a cold bottle of beer waiting for him at home. Along with the rest of the twenty-four he'd loaded in the refrigerator this morning. To replace the twelve-pack he'd made it through yesterday.

He'd have a beer and bring Sammie over to throw the Frisbee in the field. She'd play with him.

And she wouldn't let him down, either. Not ever.

"You coming to the party at the Montfords the end of the month?" Ben asked when the two men reached their vehicles.

"I was planning on it. Can't let Cassie face the town at her former in-laws' house alone."

Getting into his truck, Ben stopped. Frowned. "Cassie? Aren't you coming with Randi?"

"No," Zack said. He and Randi had never even discussed the party.

Of course, the invitation hadn't come until yesterday.

Eyes suddenly filled with understanding, Ben nodded, got in his truck and rolled down the window. "Work it out with her, man," he said as he drove off.

Zack watched the truck disappear down the street and turn the corner, cursing his friend. Didn't Ben know he would already have done that if he could?

"I'M SO SORRY about the other night...."

"I'm sorry about the way we ran out the other night...."

Barbara and Randi both spoke at once as they approached each other from opposite ends of the food court in Fashion Square Mall in Scottsdale, where they'd decided to meet for lunch. The place was an old favorite. As teenagers, they used to slip away to the upscale mall whenever things got overwhelming, for a few hours of just being normal kids. They'd walk around, look at all the girls coming and going in the latest fashions, giggling, wearing way too much makeup, flirting with the boys they professed to hate. She and Barbara would talk about how glad they were to be spared all that foolishness. And they'd eat greasy, bad-for-them steak sandwiches, usually splitting an order of fries.

Without any discussion, they walked to the steak-sandwich place, getting in line. Only three people ahead of them. But then, it was a Tuesday afternoon. Not the mall's busiest day.

Barbara, dressed in golf shorts and a polo shirt bearing the emblem of one of her sponsors, smiled as a fan hurried toward her. She signed an autograph and then slipped in between Randi and the pillar next to her, blocking herself from further approaches.

"Sorry," Randi said, "I guess coming here for old times' sake wasn't a good idea."

"Don't worry about it," Barbara said. "I wanted to come here, too. But I was surprised you could get away in the middle of the day."

"It's spring break," Randi said. "I'm on vacation."

A vacation she'd been hoping to spend with Zack. That hadn't happened, but at least her white picket fence had been put up the day before.

It was going to start making her feel better very soon.

"I really am sorry about the other night," Barbara said, looking sideways at Randi.

"You have nothing to be sorry for," Randi told her. "It was good enough for Ripley's *Believe It or Not*," she said. "Or *Candid Camera*. Hell—" she went on with her nonsense because anything else would hurt too much "—we could write a script for daytime television."

With one searching glance, Barbara swore. "He was a jerk about it. The man's a jerk. I just knew it. He hurt you."

"No!" Randi said, though she wasn't sure how many of Barbara's accusations she was protesting. "He's not a jerk, Barbara. He's a good man. One of the best. Caring and honorable. Sexy as hell—not that you'd care about that," she added with a grin, keeping things manageable as always.

Barbara didn't share her humor. "Dawn cried off and on all weekend."

So had Randi. But nobody was going to know that.

"He's just confused, Barbara," Randi said, moving up in line as the person in front of them stepped up to the register. "And he has a right to be. It's not every day a man walks into his bedroom to find out his wife's a lesbian."

Barbara was silent, although the stiff lines of her face showed her tension. She hadn't escaped from any of this unscathed, as Zack seemed to believe.

"Dawn still regrets the way she told him, just dropping it in his lap out of the blue like that."

"I think that's part of what's making it so difficult for him to move on," Randi said, feeling guilty for doing just what Zack had said she would—and just what he hadn't wanted her to do: talk to his ex-wife's lover about him. "If only he'd had some time to feel they'd tried, a chance to understand, to be a part of the decision. It's so hard when something happens and you can claim absolutely no control.''

Barbara nodded. ''Like your accident,'' she said softly, her eyes sympathetic.

Well, yeah. Maybe. Randi hadn't really thought about it.

It was time to order. Randi focused on the issue at hand. Steak with no onions on white bread. And her own order of fries.

''All I know,'' Barbara said as they found a table and sat down with their trays, ''is that Dawn won't be happy until they get this resolved. She misses Zack. He was her best friend for a lot of years. And like you, she says he's the greatest guy she's ever met.''

If Randi hadn't seen the love—the need—in Dawn's eyes as she'd looked to Barbara for strength the other night, she might have been jealous. As it was, she felt a strange sort of kinship with Zack's ex-wife. They both knew what a treasure he was. And were both mourning the loss of him in their lives.

''He recently told me that she packed up all his stuff, put it in storage for him.''

''Did he also tell you he hasn't touched a stitch of it?''

''Yes. He said it's been there almost a year. That she cleared out the house all by herself.''

Barbara nodded. ''She wouldn't even let me help.''

"And that doesn't bother you?" Randi asked, meeting her friend's gaze.

"No." Barbara shook her head, smiling the most peaceful smile Randi had ever seen. "No one's going to change what Dawn and I share," she said. "Besides, I want her to be happy more than I want her with me. Whatever it takes. And if that means she has her memories, then she has them."

"What if it means she goes back to him?" Randi asked, not because she thought for a minute Dawn would, but because she couldn't stop herself from testing the bounds of Barbara's faith.

"It won't happen," Barbara said with a confidence Randi admired. "But if it ever did, I'd wish her well. I've never felt this way before, Randi. It goes beyond Dawn and me living together or having a relationship. It's love in the purest sense. I can truly put her first." Barbara looked down, then chuckled, obviously embarrassed. "It's a new one for me," she admitted sheepishly. "And it's odd as hell, I can tell you that."

This time it was Randi who didn't join in the laughter. She envied her friend.

And listening to Barbara, recognizing the feelings she was describing, she knew something else, too.

There was no more denying it.

She was completely in love with Zack Foster. A man who'd lost his faith.

TWO DAYS LATER because she was strong, capable and in control, Randi put on her in-line skates. She'd been skating alone for ten years. She enjoyed it. She could do this.

And she'd be damned if she'd stop because of Zack Foster. Or his absence. She wasn't going to let him do that to her.

Her legs hurt. She should have stretched before starting out. The road was rough, too. Her wheels didn't glide as easily as she was used to. Or she wasn't pushing off hard enough.

The air still felt good in her face, though. And waving at her neighbors lifted her a bit. She belonged here. Was part of a community—more like a huge family. She'd never be truly alone, because she had Shelter Valley.

The elementary/junior high was straight ahead, and Randi decided to turn off. To avoid it. The place reminded her of Zack. Of their runs around its perimeter.

The turn came up too quickly; it would've been too sharp. Now she had to go through the school grounds whether she wanted to or not. And once there, she was damned if she'd let Zack scare her away. She'd skated these sidewalks long before he'd come along. And she'd skate them again. This was her turf. Her town. He was the interloper.

Oh, shit. He was also out there in the middle of the field, throwing a Frisbee for Sammie.

Head down, Randi found a burst of energy, intent on getting out of their line of vision before he saw her. In a town the size of Shelter Valley, they were going to run into each other. But it didn't have to happen yet. It had been only six days since he'd walked out of her life. She deserved a little more time.

She hadn't told anybody yet that she was no longer seeing him. Had skipped Sunday dinner with her family over the weekend so she wouldn't have to answer any questions.

She felt a rush of relief as she made it past the field and around the corner of the school, cutting across the empty parking lot. Or was that disappointment? No. It was relief. These were tears of relief in her eyes. They were also the result of the wind blowing up dust. True, there wasn't much wind. But in the desert there was always dust, she told herself. You didn't have to see it to know it was there.

Something was coming up behind her. Heart in her throat, Randi poured on the speed. She was in Shelter Valley. These things didn't happen here. She could hear the thudding behind her, but couldn't make it out. It was too light to be a man. And didn't sound like a normal gait, either.

But she couldn't mistake the heavy breathing.

Leaving the deserted school grounds behind her, Randi skated as hard as she could up the street toward houses she knew. Doors she could knock on for help. She was halfway up the driveway of her high-school English teacher's white frame house when, in her peripheral vision, she caught sight of her pursuer.

Turning her feet out, Randi circled the dog, grinning. Breathing. And still crying.

"Go home, girl," she said, and headed back out to the street.

Sammie, as stubborn as her owner, didn't pay Randi's word any heed. No matter how many times Randi yelled at her, cajoled her, commanded her, the dog continued to trot at her heels. If Randi sped up, so did Sammie. When Randi slowed, the dog did, too.

At first she'd been certain Zack would appear any second, then realized there was no way he could've kept up with them. He was on foot. Not on skates. And by the time he'd managed to get from the field to the Explorer he'd left parked on the road, Sammie would've been around the corner after Randi and long gone.

Which meant he was probably waiting for Sammie at her house.

Or out combing the streets looking for them.

Which left her nowhere safe to go.

Slowing, figuring the poor demented dog must be exhausted, Randi eventually skated up her own street. If he was there, she'd skate right by him and go into her house, leaving him to take his dog home.

And if he wasn't there yet, she'd leave Sammie outside watching for him. Either way, she didn't have to speak to him.

She wasn't ready for that. Not yet.

Not with tears streaming down her face.

ZACK WASN'T THERE. And Sammie, barking her fool head off at the door, refused to wait outside.

"Okay, but this doesn't mean anything and you'd better be good," she said, stepping aside to allow the dog entry. "You have to stay right here on the tile."

Randi needed these two, dog and man, out of her life. She'd always been in control, dammit! Was used to having people listen to her when she spoke and do what she said. She was the boss in her little corner of the world.

She didn't have any idea how to communicate that piece of information to a dog.

In her house, sitting on the floor of her foyer because it was the only way she could get Sammie to stay there and not risk getting dog hair on her carpet, Randi leaned her head against the wall and gave in to the memories she was just too exhausted to keep at bay.

That first meeting, when Zack had refused to cancel the pet-therapy club, her defeat on the basketball court, the lost races, the ribbing, the time he'd left her alone in the nursing home with Sammie—the list went on and on.

As she sat there, one thing became very clear. Zack Foster stood up to her. He was one of the few people in her life who had ever done so.

And it was part of the reason she'd fallen so completely in love with him. He'd given her companion-ship, brought her intense sexual pleasure, taught her a lesson or two; he'd also earned her respect.

She relived it all. Right up until that last night. She put a stop to things then. Refused to acknowl-edge the pain that was waiting to suffocate her.

Sammie, lying on the tile beside her, laid her head on Randi's outstretched leg and sighed.

Fresh tears dropped from Randi's eyes onto the dog's fur. If Sammie noticed, she didn't seem to care. She just lay quietly, unthreatening, as Randi ran her hand along Sammie's back, taking comfort from the warmth of the body pressed against hers.

She wasn't alone.

At that moment Sammie's presence was the only thing that kept her going.

And suddenly that last night with Zack slipped past her defenses, filling her mind with memories and her heart with pain.

Not you, too. Zack's words screamed through Randi's mind, like the painful screech of iron wheels on a train track, refusing to be quieted.

His words, the judgment he'd passed on her, was a crushing blow. She'd thought he was different. That he saw inside her, that he'd believe her. But he'd compared her to Dawn, claiming that, like Dawn, she'd chosen Barbara over him. Randi's words, her defense and explanations, had fallen on deaf ears.

It was the past careening toward her, a speeding

locomotive, its lights bearing down, mesmerizing her where she stood, blinding her. She could hardly see, couldn't think, merely sat there on the floor, shaking with panic.

Her entire life she'd been fighting stereotypes— the spoiled baby sister, a daughter of Shelter Valley, a female athlete. She'd steadfastly ignored what others had to say about her, whether they were writing in national newspapers or right here in her hometown, among the gossips. She'd insisted nothing *they* said could possibly matter.

"But it did matter," she said now, so softly she wasn't sure she'd said the words aloud. It was all so clear, in that heart-stopping instant, as she looked at those years speeding toward her, ready to crush her. It *had* mattered what they'd said, what they'd thought. There'd been so many misconceptions, so many hurts, and she'd pushed each one away, pretending it had never touched her.

They had said she was too spoiled, too pampered to make it big. That her brothers weren't going to be able to make the world right for her once she left Shelter Valley.

In fact, the guys had never made her life easy. She'd thanked God many times for how hard her brothers had been on her, teasing her mercilessly, scoffing at her high-reaching dreams. Because they'd made her strong. Strong enough to do everything she'd boasted to them, in her self-righteous little-girl haughtiness, that she was going to do.

They had paired her up with other women, simply because she was an athlete. Tarnishing the sweet innocent spirit of romance and loving, the dreams of finding a warm and caring man someday, one who was strong enough to take her on, confident enough to keep her. Forcing her into a relationship with Sean when she wasn't ready, when she didn't love him, simply to refute the rumors.

They had made her feel so violated she'd almost quit the circuit.

And after the accident that had stolen her career, *they* had said she wasn't ever going to be the same. That something inside of her had died.

And maybe *they* were right. But how could she live, knowing that about herself?

By pushing all of *them* away, that was how.

"But I *wasn't* pushing them away," she explained to the dog who raised her head to stare up at her, as though she treasured every word Randi said.

"I was pushing *me* away." Away from the words, the thoughts, the opinions, the pain. She'd pushed herself right into her always lighted, beautifully decorated little house on Shining Way. Barricaded herself so that nothing could hurt her again.

And when that hadn't been enough, she'd ordered a white picket fence. Another boundary between her and *them*.

What was it she'd said to Barbara? Something about how hard it was when things happened and you couldn't claim any control. She'd been referring to Zack and the way he'd been told about the end of his marriage. Barbara had turned Randi's words right back on her. Said Randi's accident had done the same thing to her.

"Is that what this was all about?" she asked Sammie, almost convinced the dog could understand her. Might even answer if Zack could teach her to speak English. Instead, Sammie lifted a paw, put it on Randi's lap.

"Surely this isn't a result of my own need for control."

Another paw on her lap.

The accident had taken the control of Randi's life away from her. Had she compensated for that with her carefully crafted home, her insistence on a white picket fence, her stubborn inability to acknowledge any kind of fear? Like refusing to admit that she was scared to death of dogs? *And of being alone?*

Sick, trembling, Randi hardly noticed when the rest of Sammie's body arrived in her lap. She knew only that she was relieved to find something warm, something she could hug, when the tears came anew. Anguished, frightened, weary tears that wracked her body and left her weak.

SEEING HER AGAIN split his world wide open. Zack had been so busy standing like an idiot in the middle of the schoolyard, staring as his ex-lover skated past him, completely oblivious to anything else, that he'd missed seeing Sammie dart after her until it was too late.

His completely disloyal canine had already been rounding the corner of the school building when Zack called her. She either hadn't heard him or had chosen to ignore him.

He'd run after her, but he'd gotten such a late start and Randi had such an advantage with the skates, he hadn't had a hope of catching them.

After a moment of useless sprinting, he'd given up, walking slowly back to the schoolyard, feeling as though he'd been hit by a truck. His entire body ached with needing her. With lack of sleep. With tension.

He'd have to run by her place at some point to pick up Sammie. But he wasn't ready yet. She wouldn't let anything happen to his dog. After their pet-therapy visits, he knew that much. So there wasn't any real rush.

The more he thought about it, the less rushed he felt. He liked the idea of a member of his family being with Randi. In her home.

Maybe it would do Randi good to have a dog in her house for a while. Once it quit driving her crazy. She'd be watching her carpet every second. And probably covering the furniture, too. But he'd bet money she'd also find Sammie much more of a comfort than the lights she always left on in that house.

Zack was almost home before the spurt of energy that had brought him there dissipated.

She'd looked wonderful, her slim muscular body well-defined in the cycling shorts and top she'd had on. Even with the knee pads and wrist guards, she'd looked completely feminine to him.

And seeing her unexpectedly like that, after a week of trying to convince himself of many things that weren't true—like the notion that he was getting over her, that she wasn't vital to him—Zack had to face reality.

He needed her. *He needed her.* There, he thought, leaving the Explorer in the driveway and walking slowly up to his house. He'd admitted it.

And the sky hadn't fallen in. He was still standing. Still capable of unlocking his front door, heading inside, grabbing a beer. Still capable of thought. Of motion. Still himself.

And with that shocking discovery came another. He'd been an ass. He'd been wrong. He'd wronged Randi.

It was something he'd known all week. Something he'd regretted five minutes after he'd walked out her front door that last time.

It had taken him this whole week to really hear what Randi had been trying to tell him. That his own fears were the problem. Dawn's choices were all about Dawn, Randi had said. They had nothing to do with him.

And the whole situation didn't have anything to do with Barbara Sharp, either. It had to do with *him*, and the fact that he was letting a broken relationship prevent him from loving again. Letting it cripple him…

Randi wanted faith; he'd give her faith. But more, he'd give it to himself. He'd be the man he knew he was capable of being, the man he'd always expected himself to be.

He had to go and see his ex-wife. Now.

Decision made, Zack changed quickly out of the shorts he'd been wearing to play with Sammie and into a pair of jeans and a T-shirt. It was going to be dark soon, and he had a drive ahead of him.

The things he'd done, the words he'd said, were haunting him. With the insight Randi had given him six nights before, he could see clearly where he'd gone wrong.

And where his chance lay to make things right.

It might be too late for him and Randi. But he had to do this for himself.

Just as he was grabbing his keys, he heard her Jeep in the drive. Everything he was going to say to her clamored for release. Her car door opened, Sammie jumped down, the door closed and Randi was gone.

She'd dumped him—and she'd dumped his dog.

He let Sammie in, forgoing any kind of chastisement. She'd disobeyed him, true, but he figured she was responding to a higher authority. He grinned.

Randi didn't know he needed her to wait for him tonight. And that meant he had to hurry.

LIGHTS WERE STILL ON when he pulled up in front of her house with its white picket fence three hours later. Almost midnight. But he'd already made up his mind to wake her if she'd gone to bed. Even if she didn't want to renew their relationship—if the past week had shown her that she really was happier alone—he still had to talk to her. Now. She was the only person in the world who could understand this strange tangle of emotions....

And she deserved to know what had happened this evening.

Not wanting to startle her by pounding on her door this late at night, he called her from his cell phone.

"I'm out front," he said. "I'm going to be knocking at your front door right about—" he paused "—now."

He rapped twice.

The door opened and Randi stood there, in another one of those tank tops that should be illegal and a pair of the shortest gym shorts he'd ever seen. He was going to have to talk to her about the way she dressed. It was fabulous for him. But he wasn't happy about the idea of sharing.

Not that she'd pay one bit of attention to what he said if she didn't want to.

Standing back silently, she waited and closed the door behind him. A bit confused, he looked at her, wondering why, after a week of silence, she seemed to be expecting him.

"Did Barbara call you?" he asked. They'd said they wouldn't.

"Barbara?" she frowned. "No. Why? Is something wrong?"

"No."

They stood there staring at each other, and Zack had the distinct impression that they were both expecting something. He just wasn't sure what she expected.

"Can we go into the living room?" he asked.

Then again, if she wasn't impressed with his self-discoveries, if late turned out *not* to be better than never, maybe he should be closer to the door.

"Sure." She seemed nervous. Less confident than he'd ever seen her. Oddly enough, her nervousness gave him strength.

She must need him a little bit if she was this uncertain.

But despite all the hours of mental preparation, when he got into her living room, the place where he'd first kissed her, Zack didn't know how to begin.

His entire life lay in the balance. He could no longer pretend. The next few minutes meant everything to him.

"You got my note," she said, standing awkwardly beside the couch. "I'd actually given up on you," she continued while he was still trying to make sense of what she'd said. "It's been almost four hours."

"What note?"

"You didn't get my note?"

"What note?" Zack asked again.

She walked around the couch to sink down on the edge of it. "I attached a note to Sammie's collar."

"I haven't seen it." Zack sat down on the other end of the couch, his hands between his open knees. "I went out as soon as she came in."

"So you didn't get my note."

"No." He wished he had, if for no other reason than to put her out of her misery. She seemed so damn uncomfortable she was setting him on edge, as well. Adrenaline crackled through him.

"Then why are you here?" she asked abruptly.

Finally, an answer he knew. "Because when I realize I've been wrong about something, I have to set it right."

The tension in her beautiful face softened. "What were you wrong about?" she whispered. He could see a hint of tears in her eyes.

His practiced speech, the well-rehearsed words, were nowhere to be found. His mind went blank, leaving nothing but the stark truth.

"I was wrong not to see what I was doing to myself. To Dawn. And to you."

She turned on the couch, facing him, and leaned forward. "You mean you—"

"I went to see Dawn this evening," he told her. The words, once he'd set them free, poured out of him. "You were right about so many things, Randi. Who and what she is has nothing to do with me or with anything I did or didn't do. And punishing her for that wasn't doing either of us any good. Nor was punishing myself.''

''You saw her?'' Randi asked, her eyes alight with the life he'd found so compelling from that very first day in his office. ''How'd it go? What did she say? Is everything okay?''

''The conversation was a bit awkward, but I think everything's going to be fine. Better, I imagine, than any of us expected. The discomfort between us may take a while to disappear, but we found that beneath it all lay the remnants of a friendship that was very real for a good many years.''

''You didn't fall in love with her all over again?'' Randi asked, touching Zack with the vulnerability she was showing him.

''No. Not even tempted. How could I be, when I was in such a hurry to get home to you?''

''You were?''

He nodded.

''And you really didn't get my note? You're really here because you trust me?''

He nodded, reached for her hand, pulled her across the couch and onto his lap. ''That note didn't have anything to do with the fact that Barbara didn't know a thing about any scholarship, did it?'' he asked, giving her the sternest look he could muster.

''You did get it.'' She didn't sound disappointed, exactly, but...

''No, honey, I didn't get it. But when I confessed to Dawn and Barbara what an idiot I'd been, citing my many infractions, including the last argument over the scholarship money, I got a completely blank look from the friend you'd been so anxious to help.

"Then, with one foot already in my mouth, I proceeded to dine on the other one when I explained that it was the reason you wanted to meet with her— only to find you'd already had the meeting. And said nothing about the money."

Randi sat on his lap, facing him. "I couldn't ask her when I realized, while I was sitting there talking to her, how hopelessly in love with you I was."

"Thank God," Zack said simply. The world that had been spinning out of control for more than a year had finally begun to right itself. "I love you, too, Miranda Parsons, more than life itself."

He couldn't wait another second to taste her lips. He was immediately on fire with the urgency of her response to him. He kissed her until he couldn't breathe, and still it wasn't enough. He needed so much more.

"Marry me," he whispered against lips swollen and moist from his kisses.

She pulled back far enough to look him in the eye. "You're sure?" she asked. "Because once we say we're doing this, there's no way it's not going to happen."

"Then let's say it fast, because it can't happen soon enough for me."

Randi whooped. Jumped off his lap and stood there staring at him. "You want to marry me." She said it in that way she had of making a statement sound like a question.

He nodded.

"Me," she said, pointing to herself.

And suddenly Zack understood. Randi had her own insecurities. Ones he'd probably contributed to. Ones he'd spend the rest of his life helping to vanquish.

"I want to marry you, Randi, the woman you are right now, standing before me looking so sexy I'm not going to be responsible for what I do in the next hour, the next year, the rest of our lives."

She grinned. And maybe even blushed.

But he wasn't done yet.

"I want to marry the woman who challenges me every opportunity she gets. The woman who has the courage to tackle her fears, to dare to meet a dog and maybe even like her—"

"Sammie saved me today," Randi blurted out.

"Remind me to thank her later."

"Okay," Randi said, unusually agreeable.

"So, if we've just decided we're getting married, what are you doing way over there?" he asked. His next move would be to go to her, pick her up, carry her to bed. He just wanted to hear what she had to say first.

Knowing Randi, it was bound to be good.

"I can't think when you're so close to me, and I want to savor this moment. To really understand that we're getting *married*." She grinned. "Besides, I liked all the things you were saying."

He stood up. "Do you understand yet?" he asked, approaching her slowly.

Randi ducked away from him. "Almost," she said. "There's just one thing I have to do."

His eyes narrowed. "What's that?" He had to be on his guard with her, he knew.

"It'll just take a minute," she said, surprising the hell out of him by reaching for the phone. Not what he'd expected at all.

She dialed quickly, without thought. Someone she obviously knew well.

Zack crossed to her, putting his arm around her waist. She was trembling.

He felt her tense suddenly, as the phone was picked up at the other end.

"Will?"

A brief pause. "Yeah, I know it's late."

Another pause. "No, no, everything's fine. I just had to tell you…" Her voice broke and Zack realized she was crying.

This tough, capable, courageous woman was choking on tears. "I'm getting married."

Zack couldn't make out her brother's words, but he heard the suddenly wide-awake and unmistakably delighted tone of the other man's voice. And was filled with gratitude that he'd come to this town, to this place, to this woman.

Randi was laughing and crying at the same time,

and holding on to Zack with every ounce of strength in her. And Zack, who hadn't cried since he was a little boy burying his first dog, felt the threat of tears in his own eyes.

There was no doubt left in his mind. In his heart. Randi was really his. For now. Forever.

His world tilted again, finding a new axis. Everything in his life was perfectly aligned.

Love had a way of doing that.

EPILOGUE

BECCA PARSONS stood by the piano in the Montford mansion, barely able to contain the emotion rising inside her. All around her were people she'd cried with, laughed with, worried about. People she loved.

The room was filled with noise. Glasses being lifted in toasts, dishes clanking, laughter, too many conversations to count. Life was as it should be.

The Montfords were home. And newly alive as they welcomed their nephew and his wife into their fold. As their house once more rang with a child's laughter, that of Ben's seven-year-old daughter, Alex.

Her sister and brother-in-law were over there, bragging—Becca was sure—about their baby daughter, never to replace the daughter they'd lost, but adding a whole new dimension to the lives Sari and Bob still had to live. Her dear friends, Martha and Phyllis, both divorced, were deep in conversation. They were good deserving women. Survivors. Beauties in their own right. She hoped life had good things in store for them.

She wanted to remember to introduce Phyllis to Cassie. They had professional interests that might complement each other, and—

"How're you doing, my dear?"

Becca shivered as Will's voice whispered in her ear. She turned to smile at him, still thrilled by his touch, even after all these years. "Great. How about you?" she asked.

"I'm full."

She smiled at his teasing. "We haven't eaten yet."

"I know."

His eyes were serious as they met hers, and Becca read their message. His life was full. Full and good and so worth the living.

As was hers.

This was her town. These were her people. And Becca knew they were all dedicated to making the world, or at least their little corner of it, a better place to live. A safe haven, a place where security and love, trust and decency healed the hurts, gave hope where hope was lost, prepared the way for miracles.

"Bethany should be awake soon. You want me to go get her?" Will asked.

Their daughter and Sari's daughter were sleeping in portable cribs down the hall in the library.

"Martha's daughter is in there with them. She'll come get us when they wake up."

The two new mothers had been insisting for weeks that they were going to get sitters for this evening. But no one had believed them. Including the Montfords, who'd called earlier in the week to say they'd rented cribs if Becca and Sari needed them.

"Tory and Ben look happy," Will said, nodding

toward the young couple in whose honor the party was being held.

"I'm just wondering where Randi got to," Becca said. She'd been looking for her youngest sister-in-law for the better part of half an hour.

"I saw her and Zack slip out back quite a while ago. There's only so far they can go out there—if you know what I mean. I expect they'll be back soon."

"Will!" Becca felt compelled to react with a bit of shock, though she was secretly so thrilled for Randi she could hardly contain herself.

"We were exactly like that once, if you'll remember," Will reminded her. Becca was mortified to feel herself blushing.

"Where's Cassie? I haven't seen her, either," Becca said, changing the subject before she found herself out in the garden with Will. It would be just their luck to have Bethany wake up while they were in a compromising position, and people went looking for them.

They'd never live it down.

Hmm. Might be worth it just to see...

"She's in the kitchen," Will was saying. It took Becca a moment to remember what he was talking about. The question she'd asked.

Carol Montford came in from her husband's office behind Becca and Will, a shocked look on her face.

"Carol, are you all right? What's the matter?" Becca asked, sliding her arm around the older woman's waist.

"Nothing. Oh, where's James?" she asked, glancing around for her husband.

"I saw him in the other room. I'll go get him," Will said, but Carol grabbed his hand before he could move.

"I want you to hear this, too," she said, "and I can't wait another minute to tell someone."

"What's happened?" Becca asked anxiously.

Something good, she hoped.

"It's my Sam!" Carol said, speaking of the son she hadn't seen since he'd left Shelter Valley—and Cassie—in disgrace ten years before. "He's coming home!"

Becca's eyes met Will's over the congratulations, the growing commotion, as someone found James and gave him the news. Shelter Valley was ready to welcome home the prodigal son.

And this was what life in Shelter Valley was all about, Becca thought again. The lonely found love. The lost were found. And sometimes, miracles really did happen.

* * * * *

Watch for SHELTERED IN HIS ARMS
in May 2001, a special novel
from Harlequin Books.

Find out what happens when
Sam Montford comes home!

Presenting...

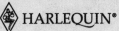

HARLEQUIN®

R_x PRESCRIPTION OMANCE

Get swept away by
these warmhearted romances
featuring dedicated doctors
and nurses.

LOVE IS JUST A HEARTBEAT AWAY!

Available in December
at your favorite retail outlet:

SEVENTH DAUGHTER
by Gill Sanderson
A MILLENNIUM MIRACLE
by Josie Metcalfe
BACHELOR CURE
by Marion Lennox
HER PASSION FOR DR. JONES
by Lillian Darcy

Look for more
Prescription Romances
coming in April 2001.

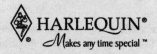

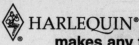

Tyler Brides

It happened one weekend...

Quinn and Molly Spencer are delighted to accept three
bookings for their newly opened B&B, Breakfast Inn Bed,
located in America's favorite hometown, Tyler, Wisconsin.

But Gina Santori is anything but thrilled to discover her
best friend has tricked her into sharing a room with
the man who broke her heart eight years ago....

And Delia Mayhew can hardly believe that she's
gotten herself locked in the Breakfast Inn Bed
basement with the sexiest man in America.

Then there's Rebecca Salter. She's turned up at the
Inn in her wedding gown. Minus her groom.

*Come home to Tyler for three delightful novellas
by three of your favorite authors: Kristine Rolofson,
Heather MacAllister and Jacqueline Diamond.*

HARLEQUIN®
Makes any time special ™

Visit us at www.eHarlequin.com   PHTB

CELEBRATE VALENTINE'S DAY WITH HARLEQUIN®'S LATEST TITLE— *Stolen Memories*

Available in trade-size format, this collector's edition contains three full-length novels by *New York Times* bestselling authors Jayne Ann Krentz and Tess Gerritsen, along with national bestselling author Stella Cameron.

TEST OF TIME by **Jayne Ann Krentz**—
He married for the best reason.... She married for the only reason.... Did they stand a chance at making the only reason the real reason to share a lifetime?

THIEF OF HEARTS by **Tess Gerritsen**—
Their distrust of each other was only as strong as their desire. And Jordan began to fear that Diana was more than just a thief of hearts.

MOONTIDE by **Stella Cameron**—
For Andrew, Greer's return is a miracle. It had broken his heart to let her go. Now fate has brought them back together. And he won't lose her again...

Make this Valentine's Day one to remember!

Look for this exciting collector's edition
on sale January 2001 at your favorite retail outlet.

HARLEQUIN®
Makes any time special ™

Visit us at www.eHarlequin.com

PHSM